The
SUMMER
BEACH HOUSE

A sweet feel-good women's fiction novel

ANAT HAIMOVICH

Producer & International Distributor
eBookPro Publishing
www.ebook-pro.com

THE SUMMER BEACH HOUSE
Anat Haimovich

Translation from Hebrew: Loba Elkan
Editing: Nancy Alroy

Contact: anat31773@gmail.com
ISBN 9798333706386

PROLOGUE

She

She interpreted everything in black and white and stayed away from the gray areas which, for her, did not exist. "Either you are good, or you are bad; either you do, or you don't; either you exist or you don't; you are either heaven or earth – you can't be both," she concluded. This was the way she saw her life, and knew she was on the correct path. She had made all the right decisions but, since they were made a long time ago, she no longer concerned herself with how she arrived at them. She simply lived by them.

I met her in the beginning of June 2010 and, right off the bat, she made a powerful impression.

I vividly remember seeing her that first time – she lit up the entire room, although, behind her warm, graceful eyes and joie de vivre, I saw an overwhelming sadness. I tried to concentrate only on technical matters, but couldn't. I had kept my distance from people for many years, finding their company unnecessary. In this case, it was different. There was something about her that compelled me to listen to her, even beyond her spoken words.

When she left for Italy, she unintentionally left behind a briefcase in which she kept all her writings. When I asked her about it, she replied, "I write during the summer. I think it's a way to help myself understand. Or maybe so I won't forget, in order to prevent making the same mistakes in the future." And that's all she said.

After a long internal debate, I decided to read her writings. "That's a mistake," I told myself as I took the notes out of the suitcase and then hastily put them back in. At last, I put the suitcase in a box and went to the post office.

"That'll be ten dollars," said the clerk.

Immersed in my own thoughts, I heard, "Sir? Sir?"

"Yes, sorry," I replied, "I'll send it another day. Thank you."

The story I'm about to share with you arises from her notes. I can't use her first name – you'll understand the reason later on – but that's only the beginning.

The following are notes from the briefcase left behind.

CHAPTER 1

07.01.2010

oday I move with my dear children to a beach house. A spacious and beautiful house.

How I wished for this day.

I really hope I won't be disappointed. I want the best for my children, like any other mother, and I am very committed to making it happen.

It all began earlier this year when, for the first time since getting married 12 years ago, I told my best friend Mal about my marriage.

My husband, Mr. B., as I prefer to refer to him, is a good man, at least I thought so, and maybe still do, I'm confused. Everyone loves him, and yet his behavior has left scars on the tiny souls of our little children. With Mr. B., society is the main thing: what'll people think, what will they say? I have no problem with society; on the contrary – but I also love my privacy, and it isn't society that determines the standards by which I live. Society is fickle. How can one build a life around something so unpredictable?

As marriage is just a formality, I presumed my husband would be my best friend. He was supposed to consider what's good for me and he's supposed to trust me, assuming I'm his best friend as well. Even if I walk by his side wearing a knee-length denim skirt and a white tank top or T-shirt with work boots (apparently an outfit that shames him), what difference should that make? What's important is that I'm comfortable with it.

Mr. B. is a good father. However, he is very critical (according to his zodiac sign) and his criticism often seems to have no logic whatsoever. At least to me. It took me a long time to realize that the root of his criticism lies in his fear of society. Again, so confusing. He is quick to analyze every situation, to try to understand it on the deepest level so that it doesn't fail him along the way. Constantly alert, his critiques are voiced flippantly and without any attempt at positive feedback so, when they are absorbed by innocent children, they wound and leave them with scars. He expects everyone to understand and accept his remarks as they come, but not the other way around – Mr. B. isn't good at taking criticism.

I'm stubborn and I don't compromise, especially when it comes to my children. From a very young age, I realized that no matter how hard I tried and how much I try to behave according to ethical norms, there would always be external obstacles. Therefore, whenever possible, I avoid them and steer away and, mainly thanks to my choices, my home will be the most protected, safe and wonderful place. Because ultimately, it depends only on me.

I am a hopeless romantic. I believe that a couple should always remember why they chose to be together, and that sending flowers or a loving message is never unnecessary or too much. The idea is to complete your partner, to envelop them in your soul, to be two but one. To take the time to do things separately as well, like girls' or boys' night, which are beneficial to any relationship. And it is clear to me that, the moment I return home, I am returning to the most beloved and safe place for me. Both the home and the relationship.

But that's not how it was for me.

I love people who tell me the truth, who tell it to me straight. That's why Mal's criticism, as well as her and her dear sister Tir's support, was so important to me. People like them help me to truly examine myself. Sometimes I come to the conclusion that they are right and, sometimes, I think to myself that they simply don't understand.

Mal is right. I lost my sense of self while trying to give Mr. B. a sense of support and friendship that was completely genuine, never-ending, and unconditional. It is not okay for a person to erase himself for the sake of another; that, I already knew. I am a very dedicated person, uncompromising in the way I choose, being sure to make the right one but, it turns out that I didn't know how to find the balance between boundless support and friendship and maintaining who I am. I didn't completely forget myself, but I lost the strength to return to myself. Mal and Tir enlightened me at that girls' night out, the one we'd been waiting for 12 years. It is so surreal to think about it now as I write this. I'm grateful for my friendship with Mal and Tir – we've been friends since birth, when our parents bought houses next door to one another. And, ever since, every summer day, we've gone on imaginary adventures that I invented after watching 'Pinocchio,' 'Marco' (3,000 Leagues in Search of Mother) and 'Lost Islands.' We went through our teenage years together, exploring the city center and going down to the sea. We tried out new restaurants, cafes, and pubs. Our friendship also stood the test of time during university, weddings, and childbirth. We never lost touch, even when various people came in and out of our lives. She and Tir have known me almost as long as I've known myself, and they were right! My zodiac sign is fire, and how can a fire sign exist without a fire within?

Mr. B. got a promotion to relocate for a time in Italy, a position he longed for, a country he loved very much, only enhanced by the fact that the Ferrari is produced there. He already had the hat, watch, shirt and a miniature model Ferrari.

He once told me, "Ferrari isn't a car, it's a work of art."

I answered, "Aren't you exaggerating? It's just a car." I thought to myself that if only he had said, "*My dear wife, you're not a woman. You are a work of art*," how different our lives would have been. He also once wanted to find a ring with the Ferrari symbol and wear it instead of his wedding ring. Really?!.

To the children and me, however, he never devoted such romantic thoughts; if he had, he would have been more accepting and less critical, would have loved us without giving us the feeling that we needed to prove ourselves worthy of his presence. It seemed as though he expected us to earn his attention instead of offering it naturally.

"We get only one life!" I said during one of our arguments, "I'm not willing to waste it on nonsense like disagreements over nothing!"

He pretended to not understand me, though I believe he understood very well. He is very cunning and always manages to turn things to his advantage, like the fox from Pinocchio who managed to outsmart Pinocchio every time by wrapping his tricks in proper and decent language, with a pitiful voice and the stance of a helpless victim. I remember when I was young, watching the whole program from start to end every summer, apparently like most children did when there was only one channel on TV. And every summer I wanted the fox and the cat to get what they deserved for tricking Pinocchio and keeping him away from Grandpa Geppetto or ignoring Jiminy, the cricket who acts as his conscience and tries to show him the right path to avoid trouble. I was mad at Pinocchio for being so gullible, falling into the traps of these two crooks without listening to his cricket friend. I used to cry while watching 'Marco,' hoping he would find his mother. And no matter how many times I watched 'The Lost Islands,' I fell in love with the lost children all over again, waiting to discover the face of the man with the black cloak. I'm not sure I remember whether or not his face was finally revealed to us. These childhood programs had a big influence on me: I clung to my mother so she wouldn't disappear on a ship to nowhere; I decided that I would be smart and not stupid and, most of all, not a liar like Pinocchio. I would obey all my mother's instructions and demands, which is how I promised myself that she would never leave me. I was the best daughter I could be. I was vigilant so that I would not fall for the trickery of evil schemers. I was bent on defending the innocent and helpless. Now I realize that I am exactly like who I didn't want to be: Pinocchio!

I fell for every possible trick. I didn't lie to others but I lied to myself, and that's just as bad. Maybe even worse, I convinced myself that nothing was wrong and that everything was fine.

I didn't listen to my heart properly.

Mr. B. said he would go 'test the waters' before he relocated us all. I was pleased with that as I knew I also needed to examine what I'd been swimming in for the past twelve years. But I haven't told him yet as I didn't want to ruin the wonderful feeling he has of fulfilling a dream. Why should I spoil it? Everyone deserves to fulfill their dream. *Love your neighbor as yourself* always tipped the scales for me, and I always chose the same wellness for others as I wanted for myself. Until one day, dear Mal brought to my attention that the sentence means you should treat others as you yourself would like to be treated. Love yourself first, not in a selfish sense.

It took me a while to digest the novelty of the idea and, unfortunately, I am not good at it yet. Yet, it comes with a price. We are created to love, every creation was created to love and, as such, I need to love myself as well. It's not egotistical. Love is a very powerful energy, everyone knows that. It is said that love is blind, it's blinding because of its power. It is true that I first have to love myself because how can others love someone who doesn't love herself? I need to work on it and I still have a long way to go. I need to understand that loving myself does not mean I'm being selfish. Only if I love myself can I take responsibility for my life; only then will I see the truth and not twist it in a convenient way that will make it possible for me to continue living the way I am.

We arrived at the house on the beach. We've been there several times before, so we should have felt completely comfortable in it. Our house in the city is a tiny two-bedroom apartment with a small sun terrace filled with potted plants, seasonal flowers and a round wooden table that seats four. I often hang laundry out to dry there, making it even more cramped.

Mr. B. always managed, very wisely I should say, to rearrange the house according to the needs of the hour, so the house was always pleasant and comfortable despite the load of things that we accumulated. Sometimes it seemed the house would expand itself for us based on the needs of the hour. That tiny little apartment gave the feeling of a spacious private house with a luscious green and blooming garden. We have always hosted: evenings with friends, birthdays, holiday meals, and some days for no occasion at all. I also made sure to invite my children's friends so that I could keep an eye on them and make sure everything was fine. Over time, when I felt confident enough, my children went to their friends as well. Despite all the effort it entails, I must say that it is wonderful when the house is full, and I loved hosting. The children used to play board games and hide and seek, as illogical as it sounds. And when they saw a movie, they got a real cinematic experience, with popcorn and drinks. It was clear to see that the guests had a hard time leaving and were already looking forward to the next visit.

It was about 9:45 a.m. when we said our goodbyes to Mr. B. at the airport, about an hour ago.

The movers brought everything to the beach house the day before. I started sorting the boxes: me, Nell, Neil, Mr. B.

Although we remembered that the house was big, it seemed we didn't remember just *how* big.

The children wanted to go out to the beach, a few steps away from the terrace. The terrace had large windows and its two very large glass doors had a wooden frame painted in a light pinkish color, very delicate. It gave us easy, direct access to the beach.

I accompanied my dear children to the beach and asked them not to go in the water: "There is no lifeguard and I need to un-pack the boxes, so there will be no one to watch you. Don't go too far, stay within earshot." I am always so practical! The boxes can wait, nothing will happen, but this moment will not come back. I stood with them for a few moments and said, "Nelly, take your cell phone with you. You know what, Neil? Take yours too." I knew it would make him very happy. We bought Neil a phone when we bought Nell hers as she entered the fourth grade. Last summer we overcame a very difficult financial crisis and, after selling a prop-erty we inherited, we were able to take a breather. I wanted to give the children everything I couldn't give them before. Of course, they didn't know how difficult the situation was. "I'll buy it for you, don't worry, just now it's a little unnecessary; but don't worry, when it'll become a necessity, I'll buy it." This was the way for me to arrange positive thoughts for them while my heart ached, worrying all the time, not knowing when I'll be able to keep my promises.

'Last summer everything finally fell into place.' At least that's what I thought because, had I known then what I know now, my choices would probably have been completely different. I couldn't stop myself from buying. It felt as if the floodgates were suddenly opened. I had been running fast in place for a long time, and when the floodgates finally opened, I was so full of energy that I ran as fast as I could, without being able to stop.

I was relieved when I finally bought them cell phones. Of course, they really wanted them, but I didn't want them to have to depend on others in case they needed to contact me.

Neil doesn't use it to make calls, rather to play his music and play games; in general, Neil is a very intelligent boy; he can easily find his way around any kind of computer or difficult game, no matter how complicated. Even more; I believe he sees the hidden.

One evening when Neil was three years old, we all sat around the table for dinner. He said, 'Grandma is here,' even though what he said was an impossibility. I asked him which grandma. 'Grandma Naomi,' he answered. I asked what she looked like. He said she had white hair. Where was she standing? I asked again, and he answered, 'Behind you.'

Nell and Neil are the most wonderful kids.

My mother, Naomi, used to tell me, "You know, you're blessed, you have very good children. You were a very good child and, therefore, God blessed you with good children." So I knew I could trust them not to go into the water and do as I asked. Besides, it was a private beach strip and there was no reason to be afraid to leave them there on their own.

I went into the house. With my cell phone next to me, I started sorting boxes, each box to the appropriate room.

I heard the sound of a car pulling up. *Have they arrived already?* I thought to myself. I looked out the window. Yes, it was the couple who rented one wing of the house. I'm not sure about them being a couple, they might just be sharing the same wing.

It was Mal's idea. She and her husband would be living in Washington, D.C. for the next few years, and she suggested that this would provide me with some extra income and, as a bonus, we wouldn't be alone in this big house.

"Hello," I said, stepping out to the driveway. "I don't mean to bother you; I just wanted to remind you where your wing is; after all, we only met once, a month ago, if I'm not mistaken."

"Hello to you, too. You're not wrong and we do remember. Thank you," Ariel replied. At least that's what I thought his name was. I wasn't sure I remembered which one was Ariel and which one was Nadav.

"Ariel? Right?" I asked with an embarrassed smile.

"Yes, yes, Ariel. And this is Prince Charming," pointing to his friend, "remember?"

"Hello, Nadav," I said, amused.

"Hello to you too," he replied. "Apologies…"

He shook his head towards Ariel as he pulled a box out of the car. "We tried… but we'll manage with what we have," he said. Ariel smiled.

"Okay then, I won't interrupt you getting organized," I said and started walking away. "I also have a few boxes to unpack."

"Mommy, mommy," cried Neil, "you have to come and see," he said.

"Where's Nell? What happened?" I asked frightened. My heart was pounding so hard that it felt as if Ariel and Nadav could hear it.

"Nothing happened. Nell is waiting on the beach, come on, you have to see," he said excitedly and impatiently. Neil is a Pisces, and the sea is an inseparable part of him. I knew the location by the sea would do him good, and my heart was so full when I realized that his yelling was enthusiastic and joyful.

On the beach, Nell and Neil found eggs of what seemed to be a sea pincer. We stood there for several minutes and just looked with a smile on our faces. Anch ran around excitedly and nearly destroyed everything, as usual. Anch is our half-collie dog, at least in appearance and behavior, but not in size. This small to medium-sized black dog taught us that we have iron patience. We knew we had patience, but this kind? We were surprised too.

I thought I should go back and continue unpacking the boxes – another practical thought?! I need to work on that. While thinking, I turned my gaze toward the house and saw Ariel and Nadav standing near us. They had come after us, their expressions even slightly serious, and they looked tense.

"Everything okay?" Nadav asked with a captivating smile.

"Yes, everything's fine, thank you," I said, taken aback by the attention and care. They warmed my heart so much. If it had been Mr. B., he wouldn't have bothered to come out; it's not like we were going anywhere, and what could be that important?

How low have I fallen for something so trivial to make me feel so treasured? I remember telling Mr. B., "It's no coincidence that the first chapter of the bible tells the story of The Creation through a speech. 'God said, and it was created,'" I once told him. "This book is a guide which teaches us how to live properly and learn from past mistakes for a better future. Right here, we learn the power of a word," I continued, getting more passionate with each word. "You're so curious and ask so many questions, interested in every issue, you want to know and expand your horizons, but you never really make an effort to apply what you learn. 'Kind words and a warm embrace show how much we care. They are the forces that create and sustain the world and everything in it.'"

I had to repeat this over and over again in different ways. Why did I have to explain the obvious? Apparently, Mr. B. didn't want to understand. I guess he wanted me to believe that I was nothing but a nagging, complaining woman. There's no other explanation for it. It's good that I'll have some time now to think, to sort things out. I am so confused.

In the afternoon, we left all the clutter and the boxes and got into our golden family Chevy to head for the city.

"Is that it? Did we manage to get you to leave?" Ariel said, chuckling.

"What's the record?" I asked.

"Almost a week," Ariel replied.

"I remember eight hours," said Nadav, who came out after him with empty boxes.

"Wow, I've never broken a record. It was nice to think that maybe I could."

"So, where are you guys going?" he asked kindly. In my heart, I hoped he would never stop asking. But then I immediately reminded myself that it was better not to get used to good things because they eventually disappear.

"To the city," said Nell.

"And we're not leaving," Neil continued. I have forgotten how powerful is a heart filled with happiness and how sad that, from just one friendly question, I am about to cry from joy.

"It's been a long time since you've been there, right?" said Ariel as he took two boxes out of the vehicle and stacked them one on top of the other, making it easier for him to lift them together and bring them into the house.

"Maybe it's better to take each one separately. After all, it's marked 'Fragile,'" I said as I got into the car and wondered how to insert the key to start the engine. I smiled, and Ariel smiled too. I started the car. Nadav and Ariel, each carrying a full box, walked down the path toward the entrance.

"Drive carefully," Nadav said.

"It's a jungle there at this hour," Ariel added.

"Thank you," I said, my heart grateful for every word, for the attention. I pondered as I drove out of the driveway – how much I missed these words, the attention. How I cling to each one of them, so happy even with the simplest kind word. I thought I was doing pretty well without them. Now I realize how much I missed them, like air to breathe. Without realizing it, I brought myself to forget how important and healthy simple, positive communication is. Now I realize that it was nothing but a defense mechanism. The breeze that now came in reminded me of what was forgotten so that it would not be forgotten again. Now that I am writing, and it is good that I decided to write everything down, I know that I won't be able to live any other way. How did I think of raising my children without it? What kind of example I have been setting for them?

We had a great afternoon. Tir and her son, Hugh, Nell, Neil and me. We managed to fly the smallest kites in the world, or so the young salesman at the port defined them a week ago, adding that it is worthwhile buying three for forty dollars rather than just two for thirty. And it was a good thing he did because that way each kid got a kite. We strolled around the lake and had a picnic in the park under the pink sky at sunset. Neil, Nelly and little Hugh enjoyed flying their kites together. It was peaceful and beautiful.

We said our goodbyes to the city, to Tir and little Hugh, and drove back to the beach house.

After the showers, Nell and Neil went to their beds, the ones we brought with us from the city, along with all the bedding and pillows, which had the familiar smell of home.

"So, what story are we telling today?" I asked. Immediately, names of different books come out of their mouths, full of wisdom and grace (I can't think of Nell and Neil without showering them with compliments, even though they will never be enough to describe how wonderful they both are). I explained that I hadn't unpacked the boxes of books yet and that I was too tired to look for them now.

"Today we'll tell the story of Snow White and the Seven Dwarfs," I said and, after some comments and complaints, I clarified, "with mistakes."

"Okay," Nell and Neil said together.

"Once upon a time, many years ago, a very beautiful queen lived with a stepdaughter and a magic mirror. Every day, the queen would ask the mirror: 'Mirror, mirror on the wall, who's the fairest one of all?' And the mirror would answer, 'You are, my queen, the fairest of them all,' and the queen would be happy. One day, when the queen asked the mirror: 'Mirror, mirror on the wall, who's the fairest one of all?' the mirror replied, 'Beautiful is my queen and beautiful is your dress, but Snow White is more beautiful than you.' The queen was so happy that she went to spin gold from straw.

Neil laughed, "No, not at all. That's the story of Rumpelstiltskin!"

"Yes, that's right. The queen was..." I start saying, but Nell immediately chimed in...

"She got angry and wanted Snow White killed."

"Yes. That's right," I said, "the hunter should have brought her heart in a box and instead brought a pig's heart."

Neil: "Not true!"

Nell: "Yes it is! According to the Disney movie!"

"And, according to the version written by the Grimm brothers, he just had to take her to the forest to kill her. Then he asked her to marry him!" I added.

Nell: "Mom!"

Neil: "He didn't propose marriage! He told her to run away," he said laughing.

"Yes, that's right, Neil. He told her to run away! What marriage? Really?!" I continued.

"Snow White ran through the woods. She ran so fast she dropped her shoe that was made of glass."

Neil: "No glass shoe."

Nell: "That's Cinderella."

"Really, a shoe made of glass?! What a mistake," I said.

"So, Snow White ran and ran through the woods until she made it to a cabin. She went inside and sat down on the chair that was way too big for her."

Nell: "That was Goldilocks, not Snow White!"

"Yes, right," I replied.

Neil: "She went into the house with small chairs."

"Right. Thanks for correcting me. Seven small chairs and a lot of mess, and then Snow White started tidying and cleaning until she got tired and went to sleep. Suddenly, Snow White heard a noise; it was the seven dwarfs. Snow White let out her long hair and blew them all away with it. She had already cleaned up their mess and she wasn't about to do it again."

Nell: "Rapunzel let her hair out."

"So what did this Snow White have to offer?" I asked.

"Maybe that she was very beautiful?" asked Neil.

"Yes, right. She's the most beautiful," I said. "The dwarves were impressed by her beauty and kept her with them. The evil queen discovered that Snow White was still alive, and hurried to grow thorny bushes and put Snow White and the seven dwarves to sleep for a hundred years."

Neil: "No, Mommy"

"Yes she did," I said.

Neil: "Not true."

Nell: "It was the Sleeping Beauty."

"My mistake, sorry, I'm very confused today. So where were we?" I asked.

Nell: "The queen found out Snow White was alive."

"Yes, and she made an apple pie and went to visit Snow White," I continued. Nell and Neil chuckled.

Nell: "She made her a poisoned apple."

Neil: "That's right, she ate it and died."

"That's right," I said, "She would have liked apple pie," I chuckled.

Nell: "Then the dwarves put her in a coffin made of glass."

"To make her tan faster," I added.

Neil laughed, "Because she died and the dwarves didn't want to part from her."

"Well? So what was the glass coffin for?" I asked.

Nell: "This way you can see her," she said in a tone implying, *Well, maybe we can move forward?*

"Yes, right, stupid question, obviously."

"Then came the prince who saw the dwarves crying around the coffin and looked closer inside and said, 'But why does she have such big eyes?'"

Neil: "What? That was the wolf from Little Red Riding Hood!"

"Yes, of course. What nonsense am I saying?" I said smiling.

Nell: "She was so beautiful that the prince wanted to give her a kiss."

"That's right! So Snow White woke up and asked the dwarves not to put her in that tanning bed anymore because, although their intentions were good, she had trouble breathing. So thanks but no thanks."

Nell and Neil laughed.

Nell: "And they lived happily ever after."

We all smiled.

They understand that 'ever after' is a happy ending, and not that they all actually lived until this very day. There is no point in being accurate in such cases. Thank goodness there are fairy tales and they are filled with so much magic. We were quiet for a few seconds.

I asked, "Who was the most miserable prince?"

They both replied, "The one from Sleeping Beauty."

Nadav suddenly appeared.

"Why?" he asked surprised, looking amused.

Neil: "Because he had to kiss the princess after 100 years of her not eating or brushing her teeth."

I waved my hand at my nose.

He stood there for another moment with his head bowed and a shy smile on his face, making us feel wonderful, as if we had renewed something for him that he hadn't thought of in a long time.

"How did I not think of that myself," he said and then started to leave.

"Did you want something?" I asked. "I am sure that you didn't make the effort to climb up here to learn about the poor prince," I said humorously.

"Yes, right. Even if I didn't want something, it would have been worth it. Now I know who is the most unfortunate prince of all. Can we leave food in your fridge until ours is ready? We plugged it two hours ago and it's still not cold enough."

"Oh right, we need to do some shopping too. That's what we'll do first thing in the morning," I said. "Thanks for reminding me." *Thanks for reminding me?? Thank you for reminding me?? Who needs to be reminded of such a thing?! What nonsense did I just say?*

Nadav: "That wasn't the intention, you know?!"

"Yes," I said with a smile, "of course you can."

"Thanks, and have a good night then," he replied.

"You too," I said. "Good night."

Nadav: "Good night. A hundred years without brushing her teeth. I'll ask Ari the riddle; I wonder if he'll figure it out," he said to the kids and smiled at them. They smiled back. How happy I am.

I stayed with Neil and Nell. I always stay with them until they fall asleep. I love my children very much. Have I already written that? Never mind, I'll probably write it repeatedly. I want everything to be good for them, every moment, every second. I want them to have a good life, everyone for that matter, so they'll grow up in a healthy world. A world of abundance and goodness. A world where people want to live with each other in peace.

Of all the superheroes, Superman has always been my favorite. I've loved him ever since I sat in front of the TV in the early 80s and saw him for the first time. Even then, I wanted him to be real and, although I was a child, I really wanted to be his Lois. Such a polite and modest hero, romantic and handsome. What more can one ask for? I would protect him from harm. A wonderful fantasy. I hoped with all my heart that it would one day become true.

A perfect world doesn't need superheroes because the people in it know it's a matter of choice, and all that's left for them is to choose what is right, fair and good. Because if everyone is good, the world will be good. Like in class, if each pupil refrains from talking, the classroom will be quiet – it's as simple as that. Why does it have to be so complicated?

Nell and Neil fell asleep. I kissed them both and left.

I went into my room, which was right across from the children's room; unlike our home in the city, where our rooms were separated by a short corridor, I could clearly see into their room; our doors were open, and we were the only ones on this floor.

I took one of the boxes of clothes to unpack and pulled out a snow globe that I feared would break during the transfer. I knew there was a chance such a fragile thing could break during the move and it was important to me to prevent it from happening. The snow globe had dolphins in it; I bought it for my mother when we were on a vacation the year before she passed away. She also had a similar trinket – a triangle with a sphinx in it and, instead of snow, it had golden flakes. Unfortunately, it got lost during the liquidation of the apartment before we sold it, four years after her death.

I stopped for a moment and looked out the window, which faced the sea. I thought about the wonderful day we had; I thought about how, despite the many concerns I had about this move, everything flowed smoothly. The children accepted the change very well. Annie, our little destructive dog who we call 'Anch' seems quite calm, especially now that she is lying on the bed, completely exhausted from 'unpacking the boxes' apparently.

I thought about the lake in the park; how before, when it was not filled yet with water, people didn't go there. Now that it was full, it attracted so many people, I thought about how much I, and people in general, like to be near water.

If you think about it, our body contains about eighty percent liquid. Maybe it needs to connect to a bigger source of fluid. I never thought of it that way. Maybe that's why our appetite always grows after being near water, especially when we go into the pool or the sea. It is as if all the liquid in our body is connected to the great source of liquid outside of us, and there is communication between them. All of this, without our knowledge, saps a lot of our energy. Perhaps that is why there is a feeling of peace of mind when we're near large bodies of water, like after a deep and very satisfying conversation. The water inside and outside of us has connected, and it seems as if we have recharged ourselves; our hearts are full, and everything falls into place.

Anyway, I find the sea relaxing and I feel at peace. Maybe I'll continue unboxing tomorrow. First thing in the morning, I'll find the box with the books. Yes. Well, then, good night to me. I turned on the light in the silver sconce with the milky shade that was fixed to the wall; after all, we were sleeping with two strangers in the house. I wasn't worried; if I were, I would sleep with the kids in their room. The truth is that I miss my Mr. B. right about now. He would be staring at the TV and I would be nagging, not without reason, of course. *Why is he staring at the TV? What kind of life do we have?* I never nagged if there was no reason to. Besides, I never nagged before; I wouldn't nag even when he sat like a lump in front of the TV. I always have something to do, so I would have been occupied, even if it was just thinking. Why do I miss the presence of this 'lump?'

Not tonight. I don't want to tire myself out emotionally with thoughts tonight.

Better I go to sleep with the good thoughts of this wonderful day. A second passes and I find myself getting out of bed, checking again that this walkie-talkie works. "Come here, Annie," I whispered. Anch follows me to the kids' room and I give her one talkie to mess with, I go back to my room and, great, it works. "That's it, Anch, thank you," I said. I returned the walkie-talkie to its place and went back to bed. The cell phone rings! Where did I put it? I didn't want it to wake the kids… I'm not in our home, ah, found it, it's almost midnight, probably a mistake. No. It's Mr. B.

Mr. B.: "Well? Did everything go well? Are the kids okay? How do you feel?"

To all his questions I answered 'fine' because really, everything was.

"How about you? Is Italy as beautiful as they say?"

Mr. B.: "I didn't get to see much but, from what I've seen, it is very beautiful. The company is nice; everything here is so different from home."

"For the better?" I asked.

"Yes, look, it's only the first day, but it feels different; it's Italy; what could be bad?"

"How's the apartment they gave you, nice?"

Mr. B.: "Yes, and the view is very peaceful. The truth is that everything is great. You sound tired." He sounds quite alert. Well, it is very exciting, I'm sure. A new place, a dream come true, I can hear it in his voice. I also know that we're missed, but I won't ask because he'll probably say no and I'll get angry. He thinks it's funny to be annoying, and he does it so naturally.

"Do you miss us?" *What's wrong with me?? Why did I just say that??*

Mr. B.: "No."

Well? Didn't I say that's what he would say? So why did I ask? I became intolerable really, I didn't used to be like that!

Mr. B.: "Okay then, we'll talk tomorrow, on the computer, if you can arrange it."

"Fine."

Mr. B.: "Sil?" A nickname we call each other.

"What?"

Mr. B.: "Sil? Is everything okay?"

"I'm just tired. Good night. We'll talk tomorrow."

Mr. B.: "What happened?"

"Nothing happened." Why is he asking? Did he want something to happen? It's good that we're far apart; suddenly the things that were hard for me to notice because of all the arguments have become clearer.

Mr. B.: "Sil, what happened?"

"Well, nothing happened," I replied. He's really annoying. Why does he complicate things that weren't complicated to begin with?

Mr. B.: "Sil?"

I don't answer.

Mr. B.: "Sil? Well, of course, I miss you."

"So was it so hard to say from the beginning?" I answered a little annoyed. I didn't want to sound angry. After all, he's in another country and I want things to be good for him there. Why did I answer 'only a little' annoyed? I should have been very angry! Even though he's in another country, I'm always thinking about his well-being. Does he care about mine? It's good that I chose to write, it helps me organize my thoughts. It's liberating.

Mr. B.: "But it is obvious, so why ask?"

"Because it's nice to hear you say it. If you had said it yourself, I wouldn't have had to ask, right?" I replied. He knew I was waiting for him to say it, and he deliberately didn't... why?

Mr. B.: "Well, I miss you all," he said in a deep voice, and I knew that it was hard for him to be far from us. Although I could hear in his voice how hard it was for him, I knew if we were closer, it would be unbearable.

We said 'good night' five more times until we hung up.

CHAPTER 2

07.02.2010

I woke up late. It's almost eight in the morning. I rushed to the kids' room to make sure they didn't wake up, and they didn't! Great. They were so tired from yesterday. I usually get up at five a.m.

Why at five? To get as much done as possible before the children wake up, so I'll be available for them when they do. Last summer I got up every day at 5 a.m. to take a walk, then came back and organized everything before the kids woke up. Getting back in shape made me feel wonderful. Finally, something I chose to do for myself, although I didn't achieve the main goal as I didn't lose any weight.

I'd come back from my walk and eat. Eating is really a comfort, however, emotional eating was unfamiliar to me. Since I never needed a diet, I had a hard time with restricted menus. The choice was made for me and, without the possibility to choose, I withered; I felt that my free will was taken from me. Even if I didn't admit it then, that was the reason I couldn't bring myself to follow the program, even though it was a means to an end. I took it upon myself to make a decision. At least this choice would be mine, full-heartedly. I owed it to myself, as insignificant as that choice may seem. I needed to decide if I wanted to go back being as thin as I was before the births of my children or stay in my current state. I decided to shed the extra pounds because it wasn't me and it's not the same energy. Anyone who knew me from the past couldn't refer to me as thin, and certainly wouldn't suggest I eat something.

I finally went from 135.8 pounds to 102.8 pounds. What led me to the subject of weight?

Oh yes, so that's the reason I took walks in the early mornings last summer.

Years ago, on summer vacation, before the children were born, I used to wake up every morning with Mr. B. to keep him company before he went to work. I used to do the same for my mother.

My beloved mother worked in the nursery at the hospital shortly after I was born. Years later, when I went to high school, she got promoted to the delivery room. She used to work shifts, quite a few on Saturday mornings. I would get up at six a.m. Regardless of how tired I was, I set my alarm to wake up and sit with her while she had her coffee so she wouldn't be alone before leaving for work. She didn't like it. "Why aren't you sleeping? It's Saturday!" she'd say angrily. I thought she was worried about me and wanted me to get my rest on the weekend, but kept getting up even though I knew she frowned upon it. I always sat down with the drink I made for myself, a smile on my face, even though I would have gladly gone back to sleep. Today I understand that her frown was not out of concern, but rather because of her desire to have a quiet moment to herself. I wasn't being helpful by getting up with her. In fact, I was interrupting. Too bad I didn't realize it then. It's sort of ironic, though, when I think about it now; I would get up every Saturday to make sure she wasn't lonely when, in fact, all she wanted was to be alone! I'd just sit there quietly next to her in the kitchen as she drank her coffee until she got up and went to work. I loved my mother very much and I wanted her to have the best. Anyway, now or, more accurately, last summer, during the holidays, I did the same with Mr. B. so he wouldn't be alone before going to work. Interestingly, for some reason, Mr. B. used to say, "Why do you get up so early? You're on vacation." Today I know he wasn't concerned for my well-being at all.

I put on Annie's harness; not a collar, but a strap that is worn from the neck and under the front arms/paws; I prefer to refer to them as arms. We walked out from the glass door at the back of the house to the beautiful strip of beach that lies tranquilly beyond it, pretty as a painting. It was a beautiful morning, a peaceful one that whispered of a new beginning, perfection. The wind blew tenderly and the sound of the waves could be heard by every attentive ear and longing soul... it was a particularly exhilarating feeling. I don't think Anch liked it though. She wasn't comfortable sinking into this wonderful white sand or wetting her little feet in the sea. It took this little lady a long time before she was kind enough to relieve herself. I hurried back to the house, despite leaving a note for the children and taking my cell phone. I also had the house within eyesight the entire time, but I prefer to be there when they wake up.

I'll make summer cookies today. I completely forgot about them! Really! We have cookies for every season. I bake these on the last day of school as a sign of the coming of summer break. These are very tasty sugar cookies with a special addition that I add to the original recipe. I also replace margarine with butter and white sugar with brown sugar. I was actually very pleased with myself. I usually stick to the instructions in recipes, but I tried and succeeded. These can be made in all kinds of interesting shapes; the ones we love the most are the hearts and flowers.

"I'm going to make myself a drink, do you want one?" I heard Nadav asking in a whisper from the corridor.

"Ari?" continued Nadav.

"Without sugar! Don't forget this time, ok?" Ariel whispered back as he, too, was trying to be as quiet as possible.

"I'll try. You're consistent with that 'no sugar' in the coffee."

"I told you I had my reasons. Don't get smart. Okay?" answered Ariel from the room.

"I'll do my best," Nadav said.

"Hi, good morning, we thought we were the only ones awake," Nadav turned to me with a warm smile.

"Good morning to you too," I said, embarrassed. I hadn't woken up in a house with a man other than Mr. B. in 14 years. It felt weird but, nevertheless, interesting and cozy. Different energies, easy to get used to. I can't wait till tomorrow morning.

"I'm making coffee. Would you like one?" asked Nadav.

I really wanted to say yes. "No thanks. I need to get ready and go shopping, I need to fill my fridge and cupboards." Why? Why 'no thanks?' It would have been so nice. Why did I say no?

"I'll clear the space for you," I said, walking away with a shy smile on my face.

"Well, it'd be very difficult to move in the kitchen, with all the place you take up."

"Have a great day," I returned with a smile and walked away.

Nadav is very handsome. Sorry, but he really is; I'm not blind. About six-foot-three, long smooth hair in shades of brown, not long enough for a ponytail, though. He has brown-green eyes. In fact, the most beautiful aspect of those eyes was their penetrating gaze, which made you feel you have nowhere to go unless you tell the truth, the whole truth and nothing but the truth.

"Have a great day," he replied.

"And remember, no sugar," I smiled again and left. What? What? What was the 'and remember, no sugar' for? I tried to be funny and came out a nerd. I hope they don't regret renting the wing; it's better if I don't talk at all. I am not sure that I'm good at small talk; I don't know if I ever was.

Nadav smiled, his smile tough yet captivating at the same time. When did I become so insecure? I started organizing the boxes. First of all, the books. I admit it's wonderful to be in the company of people who are pleasant, respect you, and see you. The energies around are not a trivial matter, certainly not a passing whim, but rather something that can change the world.

Mr. B. has a definite presence; it's just that, sometimes, when we were in a place without a window, I regretted it because, if there was one, I would have opened it and thrown him out of it, straight to the moon for a month! I naively thought that, sitting by himself, he was rethinking everything, especially about those things he was wrong about and made sure to make me feel responsible for. Too bad I didn't know then what I know now. Everything would have gone differently.

"Mommy."

"Neil! Sweetheart! You're awake! How did you sleep, honey? Good?"

"Yes, Mommy, and you?"

"Me? I slept just fine, thank you, darling." Such a beautiful soul, that boy! It's a privilege to be the mother of such a special soul. So is my beautiful and wonderful Nelly. I'm lucky to be the mother of two incredibly wonderful souls.

I grabbed him for a hug and sat him on my lap, placing my arms around his chest with his back leaning against me. It's a very comfortable feeling, as if everything is in its place, a peaceful wholeness. I sniff Neil's hair, like I do every morning, kiss him and take a deep breath. Together we looked out the open window, at the sky and sea coming together; everything was so blue and beautiful, so peaceful.

"Mom?"

"Yes, Nelly, here we are, honey, come."

"Good morning," Nelly said in a soft, pleasant voice.

"Good morning sweetie, how did you sleep?"

"Fine. And you?"

"Same."

"Come," I made room for her and hugged her to Neil and me. The three of us are sitting quietly and staring through the window. Thank God for summer vacation, for the opportunity to be together and disconnect from everything.

"Excuse me? Can I interrupt?" Nadav asked. At first his voice sounded steady but, as he continued to speak, he sounded hesitant.

The three of us turned to him.

"What are you guys doing," he asked, "picking up signals from outer space?"

"These were moments of grace, connecting with the peaceful energies of the universe which, thanks to you, have just come to an end."

"You're exaggerating, right?" he asked hesitantly, perhaps even a little worriedly.

"Not really," I replied.

"Is that so? Maybe we should move on to more earthly moments of grace by offering you guys a taste of my fairy-tale pancakes," he said with a decisive look that was not going to accept no for an answer.

"Yes. Thank you," Neil said surprised and happy.

"Thank you, we'd love to," Nell said, and then asked hesitantly, "right, Mom?"

"Yes, of course. Thank you." I replied, surprised and happy myself, but hiding my feelings of excitement. I always hide them, giving the impression that I'm just 'cool' with this, even in moments of joy and surprise. It's not hypocrisy or deceit. I don't know why, but that's my reaction. I can guess, now that I'm thinking about it and just from knowing myself, that I probably don't want to encourage effort from the other side, for them to try to please me again. I'm always careful with every step I take; I don't want to make things difficult or to be a burden. Maybe one of the changes I need to make is to stop criticizing myself all the time. All this judgment towards myself, although I've become used to it, is not right at all.

Nadav looked at the three of us and smiled. You could see that he admires what he sees. A loving relationship between a parent and her children. I could see that, like me, he sees this kind of connection as sacred.

This past year, there were days when I hated Mr. B. so much. Before that, when we were fighting, I didn't hate him, I was just angry. I wanted to live happily ever after, like in a fairy tale. The hardest part for me was not understanding. Why wasn't it possible for us? What was his problem with being a prince? It's a choice! Why does he intentionally choose not to be? It's quite simple really: Who do I want to be? What kind of world do I want to build for myself? I can build a perfect world in my private life. If I want to. It's possible, it's a matter of choice. The choice makes the goal achievable and the effort becomes easy and natural. Mr. B. felt unsatisfied, unjustly so, if you ask me. I don't think he could possibly be satisfied, not ever, now that I think about it. He had to 'eat from the forbidden fruit.' Whatever, it was his choice. Now he should bear the consequences and take responsibility. Not make me pay for it.

The more I think about it, the angrier I get with myself.

Cliché as it may sound, I believe that, with love, you can succeed at anything. Love is an emotion that grants such empowering energies that nothing can stand in its way, thus the lovers become invincible.

On one of the countless occasions we fought, during the period of several months when everything led to an argument, I suddenly noticed that he wasn't wearing his wedding band. We were driving to the mall one afternoon when I asked him why he wasn't wearing it, and he replied in a foreign, ugly tone that it was too big, it didn't match his new style. Suddenly he decided to lose weight, lengthen his hair, which didn't flatter him at all, and now there was a problem with the ring, I said it was important to me that he wears it because it symbolizes something and he replied angrily: "You may want me to, but I'm uncomfortable." It was one of the most unpleasant arguments we've ever had and, afterword, we continued arguing in the mall. Between the anger and the attempts at reconciliation, he said, "You make an argument out of everything," I said, "What's the problem? It's important to me and I'm your wife, it's not like I asked you to kill someone. Is it so hard for you to be a prince and say, 'Sil, if it's important to you, then no problem, I'll wear it?' Instead, you answered like an idiot, 'great that you want me to wear it but, for me, it's not comfortable.'" I didn't know then. Now that I'm writing it, I remember that the turning point in our relationship began when Neil was one year old – both of our mothers passed away that year. And ever since Neil was three years old and Nell was almost seven, arguments erupted that I would had never imagined we'd have.

The pancakes were really good. Afterwards, we had to hurry up and go shopping. The other tenant was supposed to arrive around 12 noon; at least that's what he said. I preferred to be home when he arrives. To greet him properly. After all, I'm the one renting him the wing.

We got to the big supermarket in the mall, the closest one that I knew of.

We loaded the cart with everything we found; I should have taken another cart. We kept piling things in as if there was no tomorrow, at least I did. I'm not being critical of myself – it made sense; after all, we didn't brought any food or supplies with us to the beach house.

As we were leaving the store, there was a dog with a collar standing right at the exit. He wasn't tied with a leash to anything, he was just sitting and waiting. I was surprised, since the closest neighborhood was quite far. It's strange that someone came this far on foot with his dog. The dog had a funny shape that seemed out of proportion.

He was cute sitting like that and waiting, but it was also sad, as a dog naturally follows his owner. Sitting like this without moving, just waiting, shows that the dog is well-trained. Training in itself is not a bad thing, it just seemed to have taken away everything the dog was blessed with by nature.

In any case, we did what came naturally and immediately said hello to the nice dog. Petting him didn't seem like a very good idea, so we gave up on that. We loaded everything into the car, or rather, I loaded everything. The children were playing with the sticker books they just bought and that's the way I wanted it. One day, they will load groceries into their car, and hopefully, they'll do it as lovingly as I do. Until then, it's important to me that they enjoy every moment of their childhood, a relatively short period that you can't get back. Nell wanted to help, but I insisted on doing it on my own; I want her to enjoy her sticker book. Finally, we all got into the car and drove off.

After I put the perishables in the fridge, we started making cookies, the summer ones:

We mixed the butter that had managed to soften on the way with the sugar and vanilla extract, added the rest of the ingredients, created small balls from the mixture and rolled them in brown sugar, placed them on the baking paper on a tray and flattened them lightly with our hands. And, in the oven they went. On the second tray, we made ones with the shapes of hearts and flowers.

The cookies were in the oven, the kids and Anch ran to the beach, and I kept tidying up. It was very peaceful and I felt wonderful. Nell wanted to stay and help me, but I rescinded her offer, thanked her and urged her to go out and play. "Thank you for offering, darling, but there's not much left to do," I said assertively. "Go, play with Neil and have fun, maybe you'll meet children on the beach from the neighboring houses. But don't go into the neighbors' houses, okay? We don't know them yet." She immediately confirmed her understanding. "Be creative and have fun."

Ari and Nadav weren't home. It was too quiet; their car wasn't parked in the driveway. I left the door open. I heard a knock on the door and turned around.

There was a guy standing there with two big bags and a guitar.

It took me a few seconds to realize who he was; I looked at him with a serious look, a little worried that I couldn't remember his name, and then it hit me: Ben! Yes, that's it, Ben!

He's beautiful, I thought to myself as I approached him. I remembered he was handsome, but not how much, apparently. Anyway, my heart was pounding so hard that I was afraid he could hear it.

"Ben?" I asked in a slightly trembling voice.

"Yes," he answered as a matter-of-fact.

"How are you? You arrived at noon, just as you said. Come on in, I'll show you around. Follow me." *Too many words, questions, sentences. What is wrong with me?*

I was embarrassed. He looked rugged yet pleasant. I felt his positive energy. He followed me with his big bags and his guitar; very masculine, quiet and polite even though he hadn't said anything yet. He matched his steps to mine and gave me the feeling that everything was fine, whatever I chose to do would be ok. I don't know why I felt that way, nevertheless, I did. I've learned to trust my gut feelings, as they're usually right. Maybe that makes me weird – I don't pay attention to a lot of things, but somehow, luckily, I manage to pay attention to the things that matter.

"Here we are," I said in a shaky, slightly hoarse voice.

I don't know why I choked like that. I haven't felt that way around the opposite sex in a long time.

Ben got the guest wing. It had its own exit to the pool and towards the beach without having to pass through the main house. The wing was bright and cheerful; its two large windows showed beautiful shades of blue sky and sea.

As far as contents go, it was a modest room. When we first met, he asked me if the room was furnished. I replied that there was a bed, a nightstand, a closet and a lamp. Without even letting me finish, he asked, "Where do I sign?" I remember wanting to show him the unit first, but he said that if it contained everything I said and it allowed privacy, it was enough for him. And that he just wanted to sign, if that's okay with me. He signed, said he would arrive on July 2nd at noon, and left. Although he didn't say 'goodbye,' he did so with his gaze; he didn't use words; he didn't need to. He also has a penetrating look, but different from Nadav's. He was more like a lone wolf.

"Okay, so here is the exit to the pool and here is the exit to the sea," I pointed out. Ben stood quietly. He didn't seem particularly interested; he just stood there, out of politeness maybe, and listened.

"You can see the bed and the closet; over there you have the bathroom and toilet. Okay, so, if you need something, I'm here for now," I said, smiling and walked away, thinking he must have seen my heart beating out of my chest. It seemed impossible not to, it was pounding so hard.

What is the matter with me? Even when I get emotional, which doesn't happen often, I am calmer than this. I am weird, I know.

I immediately blamed Mr. B. All the time with him has confused my feelings and reactions.

The wafting smell of vanilla from the kitchen was a sign that the cookies were ready.

The TV was on, a habit I acquired from Mr. B. He needs everything to be on: TV, computers, air conditioner, fan. Sometimes, if the TV was off when he came home, the first thing he would ask was why wasn't it on. I have my own quirks: I need the lights in the house to be on whenever I'm awake, I can't stand being in the dark. However, when I'm sleeping, I need the lights turned off; even the light on the alarm clock bothers me.

Of course, Mr. B. had a marvelous insight about that: "Don't you care about global warming?"

After I managed to gather myself from the surprising and confusing question, I came to my senses and asked, "Interesting, and do you care? With the TV, computers, air conditioner and fan all on?" In response, he panted and looked at me with a look that, to this day, I have no clue what he was trying to express! How did we become this messed up? Endless arguments that I didn't understand where they came from or why. Arguments that grew louder and louder and became unbearable, and I couldn't just keep quiet. Why has this happened to me? I didn't deserve this.

I heard on the news about a family in need and immediately I had to voice out loud my every thought. An obscene habit, thinking out loud; one I can't seem to overcome, but need to get rid of as soon as possible. "What a twisted world we've created in which we invented money, we print it, and yet there are those who are starving or homeless. We could help everyone in need with the money we print."

I got angry; of course, I did; how could I not? Suddenly, I noticed that Ben was standing close by.

In a soft voice, I said, "Sorry, I didn't see you there – do you need anything?" So embarrassing. I was about to offer him cookies with the hope that he wouldn't think about what I had just said. That's when I remembered they were still in the oven and they'd probably burn soon. I hurried towards the stove, again saying my thoughts out loud: "Oh no! The cookies! They'll burn!"

"Great, they didn't burn," I said as soon as I opened the oven.

"I'm sorry; did you need help with something?" I asked Ben again, who was following me into the kitchen, understanding and supportive even without saying a word. I don't think it was just me, I'm sure anyone else would have felt the same way.

He looked up from the stove and asked if it was okay for him put his drink in my fridge until his arrived.

"Of course" I replied. "Want to be the first to taste a delicious vanilla sugar cookie?" I asked as I turned off the oven, "it's hot but it'll cool fast."

He looked at me for a few seconds; I was so excited, I was sure he couldn't see it, because I never blush. Not even a little bit. It's impossible to read me. If I were to blush now, I'm sure my face would turn bright red; I would surely be exposed to a terrible disgrace.

"No thanks," he said and walked out, his face tough and serious, Clint Eastwood-style.

'Sure, no thanks,' I thought to myself. He must think I'm a complete idiot, that I have no clue in economics, not even on a basic level.

I am not ashamed of my opinions; I've never been ashamed. Even though I am not understood, most of the time. I fully believe in what I'm saying but, in order to be understood correctly, I have to explain myself. Otherwise, you might think that I don't understand anything and that I'm not connected; but I am, very much so. Sometimes they even think that I'm missing a screw, but I know I'm not; I'm well-calibrated. It's a good thing I still have my self-esteem.

I could do so much more if I were appreciated. What wouldn't I be able to do? I need to appreciate myself more.

Once someone explained to me, briefly, why it isn't possible for everyone to have the same financial start. According to this concept, 'money would lose its value.' I say that money will lose its value because of humans. A person's competitiveness and mental restlessness are the real problems. Just like recycling, not that I have anything against recycling, but it won't save the planet. It's being consumed by people, wars and negative energy. If I could tidy up the world, I would do so by first giving everyone a house without a mortgage. Alternatively, every person would get a sum of money that will allow them to live in dignity without worrying about their children's financial future. The ones who already have it will have more, that's fine. It's simple really: we are the ones who live on this planet. We are the ones who manufacture the money. There is no reason not to decide for ourselves that everyone may buy or receive a house without a mortgage, or to buy a car. As for our energy, when we are happy, we channel ourselves to good places. There are so many things that could be invented, such as a painless blood test or any other medical test for that matter. Drugs that cure easily, without experimenting on animals. Promoting space flights, from which you can see the entirety of Earth, available to anyone who wants to, not only astronauts. In short, to turn dreams into reality.

What a relief to think about it. It is possible. You just have to want it. With the development of technology, for example, we can invent machines that can do the cleaning instead of humans. The cleaners could supervise the machines from an air-conditioned office. They would be responsible for the machine, troubleshooting any problems that may arise. They would receive a respectful salary for their role, without anyone being petty or narrow-minded and questioning their worth.

We have the ability to make this a reality! It would be ideal if everyone could work in a job they love, with the choice being entirely theirs. When people are content and satisfied, they are happy; and when people are happy, they want to keep it that way. And there you have it, a better world of peace and brotherhood where, instead of worrying about how to make ends meet, people would be planning their next vacation or trip. There would be no desire or motivation for war, and even internal conflicts would disappear.

You don't buy two buckets for 12 kids to play with, it will cause problems. You buy 12 buckets for 12 children and, not only won't there be quibbling, but a castle will be built. You can always upgrade your life. Doesn't that make sense? Sounds very logical to me. As logical as it gets. What doesn't seem at all logical to me is that we have the means to produce money, yet people suffer from its scarcity.

"Ouch!" I said, dropping the tray on the counter and scattering all the cookies. I was so immersed in my thoughts that I didn't notice I picked up the hot cookie tray with my bare hands.

"You okay?" asked Ariel worriedly; Nadav was looking concerned too. Ben, who was standing on the other side, became alert.

"Yes. I think so," I replied, confused.

"Show me. Are you burned?" asked Ariel.

He turned on the faucet and placed my hands under the cold water. Nadav opened a bag of ice they had brought from the grocery store. They had just returned and, at just the right time, it turned out. Nadav put ice with water in a bowl and told me, "Here, put your hands here."

"Thank you," I said, "it's much better. Thank you." I don't think words can describe how delighted I was. So much attention, I forgot about the pain.

Maybe tomorrow I'll roll down the stairs.

Good thing I put the Biafin in one of the drawers in the kitchen.

By 11 p.m. the children and I were completely exhausted from a great day. After showers and putting on our pajamas, we were trying to choose a story for the night.

"I'll go get a book," I said.

"Nevermind, tell us a story," Nell hurried to stop me from walking away, trying to make things easier for me. Such a wonderful girl! I don't need to say anything; she always understands, makes understanding her business. No matter how tired I am, I will never be too tired for them.

"What story will you tell?" asked Neil.

"Let's see," I said, and I immediately improvised, "there once was a lady named Antarctica, and she liked wearing white. She was a very cold lady. She had a boyfriend, a cold guy as well and, oddly enough, he would wear white too. Despite their similarities, they were not close and could never meet. They were named Mrs. Antarctica and Mr. North Pole. They had other friends too; for example, there was Mrs. Africa – she loved wearing all shades of brown, that lady had a particularly warm heart. Mrs. America, she was happy most of the time; an interesting woman, that one, often manages to turn a dream into reality and reality into a wonderful dream. Mrs. Europe, on the other hand, was a little older, quieter, with one boot, a watch, and several white and green hats. Oh, and there was also Mrs. Australia who was both hot and cold, and dressed most of the time in shades of cream and browns, with a peaceful and happy blue frame. Mrs. Asia, that one was a fat and complicated lady, hot and cold and… well, there were a few other, smaller friends. All of them, despite their differences, lived together in a big round house they called…"

"Earth," Nell quickly said.

"That's right, a mostly blue-painted house, one house for all the friends to live in together."

"Did you like the story?" I asked.

"Yes," they said together.

"Which letter do almost all the continents begin with?" I asked.

"A, right?" Nell said. "Well, except for Europe."

"Yes, A." Neil reinforced.

"Well done both of you!"

"Nelly, why did you hesitate, sweetheart?" I asked. "My Nelly, you're an intelligent girl; I'm not saying it because I'm your mother," I smiled when I said it, and so did Nell, "I'm telling you this because it's true; that's the way you are. You should know that by now."

"What about me"? Neil asked. Such a sweet boy, "Am I smart too?"

"Of course you are. The smartest there is. Like Nelly, just from the boys. Nelly from the girls. You two are the smartest there is," I hugged him to me.

"I love you guys very much; you're the most wonderful children in the whole world."

"Dad probably doesn't think so," Neil said decisively.

"Yes, he keeps complaining we're making too much noise, and he is angry all the time," Nell agreed with him.

"The difference between your dad and me is that I haven't forgotten that I was once a child," I answered very clearly and calmly so that they wouldn't feel how upset I was. Inside, I wanted to say that their father wanted soldiers rather than children. The truth is, I don't have any answers, at least not easy ones, to explain what his problem is. So what if they're playing in the car and occasionally shouting and having fun? I'm happy to hear their voices, especially when they're happy, and I wish they'd be happy all their lives. It's not even shouting. They're playing.

"When you're in the car with me, be quiet, don't shout," he told them, raising his voice. They are children, this is the time to do such things – to play, to shout, to laugh, free from all worries or fear. This is the time, and they'll never get their childhood back again. Does he want to take it away from them? I wanted to ask him that so badly. Not that I hadn't told him that in the past but, this time, I really wanted to shout at him. In the end, I didn't say anything. It was a time when we were constantly arguing; he made sure to create arguments in front of the children and, in order for them to know who he was and not fear him, I had to fire back. However, I saw that it was starting to bother the children and I began holding back. How hard it was to hold back! I don't remember who said that children should know their father for who he is; he's their father, for better or worse. I used this reasoning to avoid an argument, even though I wasn't at ease with that idea. I wanted him to be the perfect dad for the kids, for the children to feel free around him. To be able to be whoever they wanted. For him to just love them. I wanted him to appreciate me for feeling that way; I wanted us to be a united front, and for them to remember him as the best father in the world. I wanted him to feel how great it was to be the best dad in the world. All it required from him was to choose to be one. I didn't understand why it was so complicated. Moreover, why didn't it come naturally to him? Without me asking for it. I wanted it to be perfect, always, for all of us. Why shouldn't it be? However, the more I wanted it, the more Mr. B. made sure to poke a stick in my wheels, our wheels. Back then, I didn't understand. I was stupid. I have a hard time with the fact that I was stupid; it's very hard for me to admit. If I knew and understood what I know and understand today, everything would have been different. There wouldn't have been a single fight.

"Mom, your phone is ringing," Nell said.

"It must be Dad," I said softly, I didn't want them to feel the turmoil inside me, "Want to answer, Nelly? Dad probably wants to hear our voices. He misses us very much. He also wants to know that everything is fine with us," I continued. Nelly seemed satisfied and happy; I too, was happy and satisfied to see her like that.

"I have to pee," I said. "Tell Daddy I'll talk to him on Skype later on." For however long I stayed in the bathroom, because, obviously, I didn't have to pee, Mr. talked to the kids, waiting for me to finish and come to the phone. Well, I had to come out at some point. How long can you pee? We talked, and the children felt safe. I should have come out of the bathroom sooner. We used to be good friends; that's the reason we got married in the first place. We stayed that way for a while. I don't have the energy today to think about what we were and what happened, I'm too tired for that now.

Later that night, just before I went to bed, I took a good look at myself in the mirror – a 37 year old woman with a small and slender body, smallish face, large brown and steady eyes, pink lips, wavy brown hair that, when it's loose, reaches past the bra-line. Craving for a touch, a look, any kind of attention. I wasn't like that in the past. When did I become so miserable?

I'm so confused! So confused. I don't mind compromising, because the means justifies the end, makes it legitimate and tolerable, and it's important to me. Nevertheless, as I write these lines, I understand that the clock is ticking and I'm no longer sure if the goal will be achieved. Or if that path is the right one at all. This compromise is not at all who I am – worse than that; it makes me a completely different person.

CHAPTER 3

07.03.2010

$\mathcal{T}$oday was a great day. We spent most of it at the beach. It was one of those hot summer days when the sky was blanketed with an impenetrable sheet to the sunlight. There was a unifying and peaceful feeling, as if all the people of the world were connected. It was hot with a light breeze; a wonderful day to spend on the beach. Ari and Nadav joined us in the late afternoon. They merged with us immediately. Those two are just wonderful – two princes.

Ari and Nadav played with Nell and Neil so naturally that bystanders wouldn't have imagined that they'd met just two days earlier. There were no fears, no inhibitions – idyllic, there is no better word to describe it. They played 'tag' and ran after Neil and Nell, then the kids ran after them. Ari and Nadav chased the children into the water and they all came out throwing mud balls at each other. Nadav and Ariel don't look like they're romantically involved. Interesting. There is a friendship between them that anyone would wish for. A beautiful friendship. If they are not a romantic couple, I hope no woman ever comes between them. I used to be accommodating to people who like to mess up things for others, telling myself not to be judgmental; they must act out of fear. They're not worth the energy, anyone could see that. Over time, I realize it isn't so. They do damage, and it isn't always possible to see them coming.

Now? I'm tired of all the spoilers. How good it would be to have another planet just for those who want to spoil life for each other; and another planet for those who want to enjoy life and live in peace. I probably have a smile on my face. I've been told I'm transparent. My heart beamed with satisfaction when I saw my children happy with these two wonderful men who owed us nothing and were there for us as if they knew exactly what we needed. I caught Ari's attention; he was already on his way to me; I must be smiling; how could I not be?

"Were you hiding? If you were, you're not doing it well," said Ari, pulling my hand so I could join their fun and, as much as it was enchanting, I was rooted to my place. They quickly picked up my speaking style and embraced it, playing with me.

I smiled sheepishly; my body resisted but allowed him to use his strength to pull me up and take me with him.

"The water is whispering: 'Bring her. Bring her to me,'" said Nadav, theatrically imitating the deep seductive, terrifying voice of Goethe's 'Erlkönig,' and we joined Neil and Nell.

"What I actually hear is: 'Give me the one with the blowing mane and eyes that become greener as he enters,'" I said in a thick voice, mimicking Nadav's style with a smile. The children burst out laughing and Nadav and Ari smiled at each other. I wasn't sure if the smile was a compliment or a 'give it up, sis.' Even now I don't know but, whatever it was, it was definitely sympathetic.

"I was thinking that we've had enough water for today," I added, having no idea why I said that, as I intended to go into the water with the children a few minutes after sunset.

Nadav asked playfully, "Want to try something fun?" immediately arousing interest.

"Yes!" Nell and Niel replied in unison.

"Let's run from here to the water till it reaches our waist; we'll see who gets there first. What do you say?"

"Okay," said the children, already ready for the race, very much amused.

"It's not as easy as it seems, so make an effort, okay?" Ari said.

"One, two… three," Nadav said, and we all started running; it was hilarious and we had a great time. On the way back, Nadav and Ari made slow-motion movements as if trying to dreg themselves out of the water. Nelly followed in turn and, once on the shore, as if by telepathy, each one of them took one of my hands. Ari gave his other hand to Nelly and Nadav to Neil and we started running out of the water. I heard Neil laugh and, as he was so thin, every muscle in his body pitched to back up his laughter. Nell let out a rolling, sweeping laugh that made my heart explode with joy; it's been so long since they enjoyed themselves like that. It was empowering.

After taking turns climbing on the floatie and falling from it on the other side, each in turn, and after playing with the inflatable tube and ball, mainly trying to stay afloat on them, we built castles, bridges and walls on the shore and decorated them with seashells. By the end of the day, we returned home satiated, although we hadn't eaten since noon. It was so perfect, like a dream. If it were one, I'd rather not wake up. I don't want it to end.

We went back to the house. Anch was jumping all around; Ari and Nadav teased the children, and the kids teased them right back. Ben walked in the front door with a serious look on his face. I don't know why, but it seemed to me that, despite the tough exterior and distancing that portrayed his lack of need for anyone else, inside it was the other way around. He needed us very much. Not that I have anything to rely on other than my feelings but, like I said, my gut feelings are rarely wrong. What a shame, all those times I chose not to listen to them.

"We were at the beach. It was really fun. We'll call you next time we go" I said.

What am I doing? *What am I doing?* His gaze didn't invite any conversation at all! Ben was watching and listening, but didn't respond. Nadav was in the kitchen with Ari and the children sitting on the bar stools around the island table. Nadav took dough from the fridge, Ari brought two trays and sheets of baking paper and, with the children, they assembled all the ingredients for the pizzas. Nadav flattened the dough; Ari mixed the sauce and smeared it with a ladle on the first pizza then on the second. The kids sprinkled cheese, corn and olives on one; Ari and Nadav did the same with onions, mushrooms and feta cheese on the other. Nadav informed us, "Dinner is in exactly half an hour. On the menu, we have: super-tasty homemade pizzas, one with corn and green olives, the other with onions, mushrooms and feta cheese plus sliced vegetables. Location: West Wing." Nadav looked at Nell. She immediately replied with a smile, "But the West Wing is off-limits," referring to Beauty and the Beast. She's wonderful, witty and so smart.

"Don't worry, little princess," Nadav continued, "The flower doesn't exist anymore in this wing, the prince has been saved," he helped Nell get off the barstool.

"You like Belle too?" Nell asked happily.

"I thought I was speaking to her," Nadav said, smiling. Although Nell is still young, she was very flattered. Nadav saw her as the princess she loved the most. The one who saved those she loved. Every girl wants to be saved by her prince. Nelly wants to save her prince right back.

"I see we've sucked you into our fairytale world," I said smiling, surprised like Nell.

"Not bad buddy, not bad at all," I heard Ari say to Nadav as we went upstairs.

After the showers, we met on the deck. The whole downstairs had the delicious smell of pizza. Ari was busy with the vegetables and Nadav was outside setting the table. Thick candles were lit and immersed in white sand, each in a large special jar of its own. I hadn't lit them in a long time. There was a warm and pleasant breeze. It was so beautiful. The children immediately wanted to help.

I took the pizzas out of the oven and sliced them with a pizza cutter. I couldn't find the one we bought at IKEA the last time we were there. It has a nice blue handle that moved in the direction I wanted. The one I was using right now was old and didn't cut straight; no matter how much I tried to direct it, the blade had its own path. I prayed it wouldn't resist this time and move the way I wanted. My prayers were answered, but it wasn't easy.

The TV in the living room, which was almost as big as a movie screen, was tuned to a movie channel showing 'The Bachelor' with Rene Zellweger from 1999.

I didn't think Ben would join us, and I was right; he didn't. Too bad I was so sure. Next time, I'll try the technique of 'The Secret,' trying to wish it true for him to join us.

Nope! I was definitely wrong! He came. No need for The Secret.

"Thanks for the invitation, but I need to go," he said. I might need to brush up on The Secret's techniques.

His gaze was tough, yet indicated gratitude. He turned to me asking, "How's your hand?"

"Fine. Thank you." I said in a hesitant voice, thinking I didn't hear well when he asked how I was. That he would even remember.

"What happened to your hand, Mom?" asked Nell, worried. Neil immediately looked at both of my hands.

"Nothing," I raised my hand and moved my fingers while waving goodbye and smiling.

"See?" I said to them.

"Have a nice evening," said Ben and, although he was serious and stern, a closer look into his eyes showed that there is more to him than meets the eye, much more than he wanted to reveal.

"Thank you. You too," Nadav answered for all of us.

"Another time," I said, as he was walking away.

He turned his head as he walked toward the door, politely looked back and left.

The conversation flowed and the atmosphere brought only peace and great contentment. It was a great evening.

We cleaned the table. As in plural... not just me! I wasn't the only one doing the cleaning. Like at home, whenever Mr. B. was on vacation or on Saturdays and Sundays. On normal days, Nell, Neil and I have dinner without him; he never makes it on time for dinner. I felt what it was like to be with other adults, which I hadn't experienced in many years. Everything was arranged very quickly but what really felt great was the sharing; one complemented the other, and it was wonderful to be part of it. Moreover, not alone.

Afterward, we all settled in the living room and watched a movie that was already after its peak and nearing its end.

"Nice movie," I said, intending to get up and go to bed with the kids before I fell asleep on the couch.

"Kitschy," Nadav said with a smile.

"Yes it is," Ariel added smiling.

"And kitsch is bad?" I asked, grinning.

"No," Ariel said, elongating the 'no' slightly, which obviously meant he was about to contradict himself, "but that doesn't mean it's not," he chuckled, "but if you like it, we're right there with you," and it seems he really meant it.

"Kitsch is good," I persist as I picked up Neil into my arms.

"Yes, but you'd have to agree with us, it's still..." Nadav said.

"Kitsch is good," I insisted. I gave Nell a hand and we moved forward.

"What's kitsch?" Neil asked.

"Yes, what does it mean?" asked Nell.

"Something simple, not complex, that most viewers will like," I replied.

"It sounds ok," Nell said.

"Only because your mom explains it in a positive way," Nadav said softly, sneezing.

"Gesundheit," I said chuckling, "since we're speaking German."

"Nicely done, ma'am – not many people know 'kitsch' is a German word," Ari said impressed. I felt wonderful. I don't remember needing compliments at all; I was content with myself and that was enough for me. It wasn't so much the lack of compliments, but the constant dissatisfaction and never a kind word that had collapsed me emotionally. And this evening made it all the more obvious to me. Such a wonderful feeling from such a small compliment. How could I have ever lived like that? I feel like a little kid discovering a new world, one which was constantly surprising me for the better.

"Really? 'Kitsch' is a German word? How did you know that?" asked Nadav, surprised by Ari.

"Didn't we agreed I was super-smart?" he said amused, "I don't remember where I learned it, but I knew it and now you do too. Keep learning." Ari continued.

"You're such an Australian," Nadav said.

"Australian?" I asked.

Ari smiled and looked at Nadav, who immediately turned to look at me, nodding his head in approval and with a shy smile.

"Well, it's late, another time."

Neil was falling asleep in my arms, his head resting on my shoulder. "Mom I don't understand, is kitsch good or not?"

"It's good, not everyone can relate."

"So it's good," Nell said.

"That's right," I replied, "it's just that the real intention of kitsch is that there is no depth, things are kept quite simple and predictable and, as such, they are not very interesting," I continued to explain as we went up to our rooms. "Well, to each his own."

We spent the next few days sitting on the beach staring at the horizon until sunset. We needed to disconnect from the world we had grown accustomed to in the last two years. One can only see that the Earth is round from a distance, not so much when you are on it – it's inconceivable that it is round, despite the proven scientific explanation of gravity. You have to take a step back from things to be able to see them with perspective. It's hard. It's scary to discover things I wouldn't have imagined could ever happen. I'm not sure how I'll deal with these new revelations.

The more time we spend on the beach enjoying freedom, the more I realized that not dealing with things is scarier than dealing with them. What if I wake up too late and I won't be able to get back the lost time. How will I be able to live with myself?

That night I finished writing a play: 'From Adam to Noah.' I also started taking my writing more seriously and composed an adaptation to the movie 'The Beauty and The Beast.' From a very young age, I would sit in front of the TV or movie screen and give my critique: Is the casting appropriate? Is it well written? Is the act convincing enough, etc.

Now I realize how much we needed the respite, from everything. As for the other tenants? I'm sure each had his own reasons. I don't ask too many questions, I don't pry. Therefore, I don't know anything about Ari or Nadav except for the fact that they are wonderful companions. When Nadav or Ari would prepare breakfast or dinner, they took us into consideration and only informed us what time to arrive, and we did the same for them. Ben was a loner; he seemed to be away from home most of the time. The few times I saw him, he would go into his wing and then come out a few minutes later and head to the beach. After that, he would return to his wing and not come out again. In general, Ben was an enigma. He was pleasant, quiet and tough, giving the feeling that he was capable, a strong backrest with a loving heart, but well-hidden. Perfect and wounded. Nothing happened that testified to any of this, but that's how I felt. I was glad he was the other tenant, and I was happy that these were the people sharing the summer with us.

CHAPTER 4

07.10.2010

*T*oday we met other children on the beach.

Ari and Nadav also came, and I was glad to see that Ben came too, although he was sitting far away from us, closer to his room.

We 'buried' Nadav in the sand.

"You deserve it," I told him, chuckling, "you're too cynical." Nadav has a cynical sense of humor, not because he is disgruntled, but rather because he is a genius with an interesting point of view on most subjects. He has a good and stable energy about him.

"Wait till I get out," he said.

That was Ari's idea. He told the children, "Nell, Neil, let's cover Nadav with sand. Teamwork?" He knows his way around kids, and Nadav, too.

"Both of you are going to be wonderful fathers," I said. My heart ached. Why can't Mr. B. be more like that? I thought it was my fault, that I couldn't get him to do all these wonderful things, but I'm sitting here, looking at Nadav and Ari choosing to be that way. I didn't need to do anything for this to happen. Only a disgruntled person does everything they can to burst a bubble if given the chance.

"You really think so?" Ari asked in a serious voice, slightly embarrassed.

"I don't think so, I know so," I replied decisively.

"He closes himself off all the time," Nadav said as he looked at Ben while the children ran into the water. The three of us were left alone, Ari to my left, Nadav covered up to his neck with sand to my right.

"He probably murdered someone," said Ari.

"Okay…" I laughed. "He actually looks like a good person."

"Those are the ones you need to watch out for the most. Aren't they?" Nadav reinforced Ari's observation.

"That isn't nice. He has good eyes and you know what they say about the eyes?"

"They are the mirror of the soul?" he asked sarcastically.

"Right?" I smiled. They were quiet for a moment, as if they realized I wasn't done. "So you know…" I continued, embarrassed as if I had blurted out complete nonsense and I wished the earth to swallow me up this very moment.

"Come on!" said Nadav, leaning his head against the sand cushion we made him, closing his eyes, a smile on his lips.

"You can be as cynical as you want, it's still true," I insisted. Beyond the fact I believed it to be true, I had to save my honor. Which now seemed deep underground.

"So what are our eyes are telling you?" Ari asked.

"You have extremely good souls," I answered without hesitation.

"See, I told you, you're very far from the truth," Nadav said.

"Forget about the eyes being the mirrors of the soul," he continued, "It's a cliché, I'm telling you."

Ari and I both laughed.

"Now seriously, one of the letters that came in the mail was addressed to Benjamin Franklin," said Nadav.

"Really? Franklin, like the founding father?" I said. "Maybe he's a descendant of his."

"They said on the news today that, due to the impact of the moon, the water will reach the roads close to the beaches. At around half past eight," Nadav said.

"Oh my God," I said, frightened. "Ari, get Nadav out! Nell! Neil!" I stood up, calling out to kids.

Ari choked on laughter and grabbed me by the hand as I began to move forward. "You're so gullible," he said, laughing. I don't recall hearing him laugh before.

"It's a wonder you're alive at all," Nadav added. He, who was sure that I would understand the first prank thanks to the second, didn't expect me not to understand and he laughed too. Thinking about it now, how hadn't I understood?

"You know? You're a real idiot," I said. "It's not true? You're a real moron!"

I sat back down. They started laughing again. "Alright, alright," I said. Nadav and Ari were still looking very much amused, "so, no Benjamin Franklin?" just making sure I understood correctly.

"Yes to Benjamin, no to the Franklin. 'Maybe a descendant of the founding father,'" Nadav quoted me. "You're very funny. Everyone with the last name Franklin is a descendant of the founding father?" said Nadav.

"Are you really Australian?" I asked Ari.

"Not really. We moved to Australia when I was a kid,"

"He's Australian," Nadav said.

"With you, we aren't speaking," I said. "What time is it?" I asked suddenly.

"7:30," Nadav said, his arms still covered with sand.

"Ari?" I asked.

Ari looked at his impressive diving watch, "7:30," he replied.

"I was right. What do you say about that?" said Nadav.

"Oh my, it's late. I promised the kids we were going to see a movie tonight and it's starts at 8:30," I said in a rush.

"We'll also come," Ari said, "if you'll have us, of course."

"Do you want to come?" I was both surprised and delighted.

"Yes. Why not?" Ari replied.

"Of course we want you to come," I replied, "happily!"

"Which movie are we going to?" asked Nadav.

"Toy Story 3. Last showing is at 8:30 p.m." I replied, "And we still have to buy tickets. How had I not noticed the time? Kids, we need to hurry up or we're going to be late," I called to them.

"I want to stay at the beach. Can we go another time?" asked Neil. This darling boy has a hard time leaving the sea. I should have started the farewell from the sea an hour ago.

"I do want to go to the movie," said Nell. "We've been waiting for this movie, remember?"

"Yes, okay, I'm coming," Neil said, leaving the sand.

"Great. We going to see Toy Story 3."

"We'll come to the beach again tomorrow?" asked Neil.

"Yes. Tomorrow, the day after and any day that you want," I said. "We're having fun, aren't we?"

"Yes, Mom," I looked at Nelly smiling. "Yes, Mom, very much."

"Ari and Nadav want to join us," I needed their approval. I knew they'll be happy, otherwise I wouldn't have accepted Ari's offer.

"Great!" Nell said smiling.

"Really? They're really coming?" asked Neil.

"Yes, they want to join us." I replied in a happy voice.

Nell and Neil seemed so satisfied that they couldn't speak at all, their eyes were shining, a shy and content smile on their faces. I know they felt as wonderful as I did that Ari and Nadav wanted to come of their own initiative. They wanted to be with them, not like with a father who says, "No, what for?" and then does come, only after taking all the wind out of their sails.

Their happiness fills me with the same satisfaction. It was clear to me that they'd love the idea, so I was glad that Ari and Nadav offered.

We arrived at eight twenty-seven and I told Ari and Nadav, "Let's split up to get to the box office." Whoever arrives first buys tickets for everyone. I didn't want the kids to be disappointed. I prayed they weren't sold out.

Grabbing my hand, Ari said, "No need, we've already booked tickets online." I wanted to hug him. He was such a good soul! I didn't have to motivate him, hear complaints or exhaust myself. He did what needed to be done. He took initiative. Perhaps these actions are trivial and natural to some but, for us, they weren't. That's why I see them as noble people. Nadav's already gone to buy popcorn, but not before asking what everyone wanted to drink.

It was a good movie, very good. I was surprised, since the first two were excellent and I didn't think they could be surpassed. Interestingly, we all agreed on the best scene in the movie, when all the friends are holding hands just a few moments before they thought it was their end.

The kids had fun. I had fun. I wished it would never end.

I was very tired and happy. The children fell asleep as soon as their heads hit the pillows. First time it's happened. We usually talk before bed, even with my eyes half closed from fatigue.

I thought about the wonderful day we had, the way everything went so smoothly and how we all complemented each other. And how wonderful it was to be a part of it all.

CHAPTER 5

07.31.2010

*G*ood morning, universe. Good morning to me. Today is my birthday. This summer it feels as if all the days are merging into one another. The children probably didn't remember. Might as well do something special. We used to have a tradition that every birthday boy or girl chooses a restaurant, or whatever activity, and we all go together. I'm not sure what I want to do. I'll ask the children what they want to do today, and that's what we'll do. Since the difficult period with Mr. B. started, the never-ending arguments which I couldn't stand, this is the first time I feel that I can give my children what they deserve, the peace and quiet and security, the enjoyable childhood they deserve. It's true that it takes two to tango, but someone has to take the first step and it was never me, not even once! He didn't want to hear or to understand that, as long as it depends on us, it can only go one way. I feel the only way I can breathe is through my children. Not as a burden, God forbid. They don't know that's the way I feel. I don't want them to feel obligated to me. However, they are my existence. A testament of who I am. Sometimes life is on hold for a bigger goal and, when you think about it, it doesn't seem so. There's a great sense of fulfillment once you've achieved it and the time it took to get there doesn't feel like a sacrifice, but rather moments of grace that offer you the opportunity to smile and be thankful, as if all the pieces fell into place.

Today was a strange day. The kids didn't want to do much. So much for the surprise plan for my birthday, which only I knew about. The children said they made plans with the neighbors' children. Ari and Nadav weren't around. Neither was Ben, come to think of it. Looks like I'm by myself today. Well, that's fine. I'll enjoy having time to myself.

I went up to the room and laid down on the bed, something I don't usually do during the day, only when I'm sick. Even then, only for a very short time, when the illness overcomes me and I'm completely exhausted. Anch jumped on top of me and lay next to me with her head pushed to the side of my pelvis and rolled onto her back. I pet her with one hand and put the other one under my head, looking out to the sky. It was beautiful. Clear with a serene light blue color. The skies must look like that every day, how much strength they give in their stillness, in their beauty. There's so much power in the silence. I've long forgotten about the sky because of all these arguments, and it's become just a sky, of sun or rain, cloudy or clear, but not as an amazing part of this complex and interesting universe. The blue of the sea is a reflection of the sky, the blue of the sky is a reflection of what? Space is completely dark, I don't remember hearing an explanation for it, I wonder what the scientists' explanation is, I smirked to myself. I wonder what my take on it will be.

I always have an opinion. And I hold it and defend it, any time I feel I'm right. Unless proven otherwise. When I learn something new, I appreciate the person who enlightened me; thanks to this person, whoever they may be, I won't hold a wrong opinion.

So what am I going to do today? Maybe I'll go shopping? We need to renew some supplies. I'll buy ingredients for delicious desserts and make a cake for my birthday. The kids will be surprised when I call them for dinner.

Neil loves waffle rolls stuffed with ricotta cheese wrapped in dark chocolate, Nelly loves it too but she'll be just as delighted with stuffed cookies. I love poppy cake, cheesecake and apple strudel. Yummy. I'll bake it all. I'll go now, as long as I'm not hungry, otherwise I'll buy everything I see. Come to think of it, I'm pretty satisfied most of the day even though I hardly eat. As for my birthday, not that I'll bring up my birthday if it isn't mentioned, but I think it would be very important for the kids after the nightmare we went through. And for what? Well, I'll leave it be, at least for today, so it'll be a special day.

I went to take the shopping bag from the closet and a photo album fell down. Two pictures fell out of it. The first one was of Nelly and me when she was three. My hair was wet and we were lighting the Shabbat candles. The second one was of Neil and Nelly asleep together. I'm not religious, but I love maintaining the difference between Shabbat and the other days, to make it unique. Back then, I must have been happy that there was no kindergarten or school the next day.

Back when I was a child, I sat quietly at school when I had to. I had no choice, but I preferred to play and, on Shabbat, there were no restrictions, I could play whenever and whatever I wanted to. The beauty of childhood, the security and love, the heart that is excited by anything new, from events both simple and big, the belief that whatever you dream is not a fairytale and the sky is the limit, so there is actually no limit at all, to see solutions and not problems. Believing is the name of the game, believing that you can do something without someone standing there to tell you that you can't, without inhibitions, without thoughts of yes or no, simply with the complete belief that everything is possible and, in good faith, you can do whatever your heart desires, even if someone else's logic says you can't.

I called Nelly and asked how they were doing and if they were having fun. They were. I asked if it was okay for me to go shopping. They agreed, but didn't want to come with me. Surprising. They always want to come with me, preferring to be with me than with others. Not that it was how I wanted it to be, but that's how it was, and I felt very flattered every time. More than that, I was happy to know that they were happy with me. It was better they didn't want to come, they would have seen what I was buying and there wouldn't be any surprise in the evening with the cake...

I prepared a treasure hunt, burying notes in my room, the children's room, the living room, balcony, kitchen and in every corner I could find. The last one should have been in the pool but, for some reason, I couldn't open the door and couldn't find the key. I had to come in from Ben's room but didn't want to disturb him. I buried it in the foyer area of the pool in front of the closed door and went to change the previous note so they would search in the right place. I put it in a pirate's box with two wooden genie bottles that resembled the ones in 'I Dream of Jeannie,' albeit slightly larger.

I Dream of Jeannie was an old show that I use to watch as a kid whenever I was sick, and I watched it a lot because I was often sick. I had pediatric asthma that developed when I was eight months old until fifth grade. It came back for a brief period during my pregnancy with Nelly. Luckily, only for 24 hours because it was a real nightmare. I couldn't breathe, no matter what I did, and I had a cold and bronchial inflammation. I was afraid to take antibiotics in case they might hurt my baby, but the doctor warned me that, if things got worse, it would be even more dangerous for the fetus.

The inhalation they gave me at the clinic didn't last and Mr. B. went with me at night to look for an open pharmacy to buy something that would open up my airways so I could breathe more easily. In the end, we found a store that sold a Chinese ointment that miraculously made me breathe better. I manage to fall asleep in the early hours of the morning, not completely lying down, on the couch in the living room. I fell asleep, nevertheless. I think I hadn't slept almost an entire day, I just couldn't. Mr. B. also fell asleep in the living room with me, on the other couch.

As for Jeannie, I used to imagine what I would do with such powers, to where I would teleport myself. I enjoyed imagining the freedom that her power would give me. Magic is marvelous, what a blessed power it is and I wished I had a magic power. To handle everything easily and make wonderful things happen. It would be sublime.

In the evening, the children wanted me to come and see something in Ben's wing. When I tried to dissuade them from it, they insisted that they saw something wrong and that I should check it. I didn't want to as Ben wasn't home, it didn't feel right going in.

"Is it Ben's?" I asked, "He needs to take care of it, it's his, and it's wrong of you to go into his room when he's not there. Why did you go in?" I asked puzzled. It's not like them.

Nell and Neil explained it was in the pool so I agree to come.

When we arrived close to the pool the whole area was very dark. "Wait a minute, I'll turn on the lights, I don't like it when it's dark like that," I said, pulling my hand from Neil's. I started looking for a switch.

"No, Mommy, come," Neil said, taking my hand, "You have to see it in the dark," Nelly said, quickening my steps toward the pool.

The pool was decorated with beautiful balls of light, like Chinese lamps only spherical and white. The trees were strung with a chain of fairy lights of all kinds, scattered everywhere, there was pleasant music that started to play as soon as I entered, and the dining table was beautifully set. Everything was meticulously organized and with great love and care.

"For me?" I was very surprised, no one had ever gone to such lengths for me before.

"Thank you! Wow!" I put my hands on my cheeks. "How did you know?" I said very excitedly. "I didn't think you'd remember!" I turned to Nelly and Neil, they smiled and hugged me on both sides. "It's so beautiful. Couldn't be better."

I stood there wearing bottle-green Levi's overalls that I had purchased when I was twenty years old and a tie-dye floral tank top.

I was amazed, taking in all the beauty that was there. The hearts of these wonderful people that I met only at the beginning of this month and found myself loving them very quickly. And the precious hearts of my children, of course, first and foremost. The most wonderful children in the world.

"Thank you so much," I said smiling to Ari and Nadav.

"And you thought you were going to keep this day just to yourself? We cracked the case," Nadav said with two glasses of wine in his hands as he approached me and handed me one. He kissed me on the cheek and pulled me closer to him, "Congratulations, honey," he smiled,

"There's no one like you," he raised his glass of wine and looked me straight in the eyes. I wanted to tell him, 'What a sweetheart you are, you're the best and I can't thank you enough for everything you've given my kids this summer,' but I couldn't say a thing, I was so excited. Everything I was thinking stayed in my heart. Ari handed glasses of grape juice to Nelly and Neil and Ben poured himself some wine. Yes, Ben was there too. I felt wonderful and special. So special, it was if they too were as happy as my children that I was born. Ari said, "We'll raise a glass in honor of a sweet little woman. Perfect mom who turned an ordinary summer into a special one for us." We all chuckled. "A woman who deserves all the good in the world and all the good she wishes for herself." I wanted to thank him so much for this whole evening, even though it had just begun. It was already more than enough, all this effort made for me, the wonderful experience my children must have had organizing this evening. My breath was taken away by the gesture, I tried hard not to cry, and all I could do in those moments was smile. Ben stood farther away than Ari, who approached me, kissed me too, and hugged me with his free hand, just like Nadav did. I felt loved. Very loved. Very, very loved. My heart almost exploded with excitement. They couldn't tell, although I was smiling and fascinated; I didn't externalize the depth of my feelings. Ben raised the glass in my honor, from afar, smiling with a smile that was both shy and stern. They must have made a big effort for me if they managed to convince this lone wolf to join the party. The evening was so perfect. It couldn't have been more perfect than this.

"Congratulations, hon," Ari said.

"Thank you, thank you, thank you," I said, raising my glass, "I'll never forget this. Ever," I said in a serious voice.

"We're counting on it," Nadav replied.

I drank the wine and was about to cry when I heard Ben approaching, saying, "I hope your husband appreciates everything he has." He said this in a heartwarming tone, though I thought it strange that he said that.

I saw Nadav and Ari clinking glasses with Neil and Nelly and approaching the dining table, all the while teasing each other.

The next few moments were a blur, I just watched, I didn't hear anything.

Not responding to what he said, I told Ben, who was still standing in front of me with a smile, "Sorry, I forgot something in my room, I'll be right back" and hurried away.

I went up to the room and my heart ached. So, so much. I was glad that the kids were having fun and that they were still downstairs. I sat on the bed and shook my head from side to side, put my hands over my ears, not wanting to hear my own thoughts. The tears flowed on their own and my heart clenched; it contracted so much that I couldn't breathe. Why? Why did he have to destroy everything? I'd invested and built our home with great love, without any requests, without complaints, for all of us, for us! Why did he choose not to see it? Raising my eyes, I saw myself in the mirror. Who am I deceiving? I lost weight because I was afraid. I was so scared when I found out he had a cell phone that I didn't know about. I was so scared when I saw the messages he wrote to another woman, messages explaining about the other phone. I was afraid that I was married to an unreliable person capable of such a thing. I thought our relationship was understood, our feelings, our goals. I trusted him so very much. There had never been a communication problem between us, before all these fights. He talks a lot and about everything. He wasn't ashamed to talk about anything, everything was out in the open, so naturally. Just when my dear mother passed away and I was left alone, he took advantage of the situation, to my detriment. How could he behave like this? Who behaves like that, anyway? You sleep with one woman by your side every night, she supports you in whatever you need, taking it upon herself to make sure everything goes well for you and the whole family. She nurses you when you're sick, strengthens you when you hesitate and are confused, she is happy for you with whatever that makes you happy, and constantly gives you unconditional love. How is it possible? You want out, fine, do as you wish, it's your life. Nevertheless, there's a proper way to do things. You could have said thing nicely and with sensitivity and, even though it'll hurt me, at least I'll have that, the fact you didn't want to hurt me. You should accept whatever I choose that will bring me peace both during the divorce and afterwards; better it will be on my terms, because mine are fair and just and will be in the best interests of our children and, ultimately, in your best interests as well. Because, unlike you, I do remember the grace of youth. How was he not ashamed of what he did? How could he treat me that way? I was so frightened that I lost all sense of self. I was mostly afraid that, when everything fell apart, my children would have to sleep outside the home they knew all their lives, and not out of choice. Leave the home I built for them, not only the physical one, but also their safe place. I was afraid that everything that was mine wouldn't be mine anymore, everything I worked so hard for would go down the drain. More than anything, I was scared that I wouldn't be able to see Nell and Neil every night before they went to bed, and what would happen when Neil needed me before he fell asleep? Nelly is 10 years old, but she's still a little girl and what if she needs me? What an injustice it will be to them, this separation, and why do it to them? They are such good children they don't deserve it! I don't deserve it! What an injustice to me! Why? For what? I agreed to anything he wanted, I didn't poke a spoke in his wheels, under any circumstances. I stood by him even when we had nothing. I saw him as a friend, I stayed by him for better and for worse, in sickness and health, for rich or for poor. I believed in those commitments, those vows, our relationship, and I had no doubt about mutual loyalty.

I was so angry at his insulting behavior over the past few months, his accusations towards me even though they weren't true at all. I didn't understand why he kept finding subjects to fight about. Why he had to disturb the peace and quiet at home. He created instability, violating the harmony.

At first I was worried about him, I thought he was having a nervous breakdown because of his career, that things weren't working out for him. I told myself that, if it were the other way around, I'd want someone to pick me up; I'd wish someone would care enough not to let me fall apart. I didn't understand what was happening, I would never have dreamed about what really happened.

I remember him suddenly coming home at 9:30 p.m., which was when he realized I'd found out. He said to me, "Explain to the children why we are separating." Suddenly, with no reason? For no reason? I was his best friend. "You do the explaining," I said, not knowing what to explain. I didn't understand the reason either. How can I explain? He didn't say anything to them. He stayed sullen, and clouded the atmosphere even more. On top of that, he had been having very disturbing outbursts recently, and I felt that if I said something it would happen again, and if previously I managed to rearrange the picture for the benefit of my memories and those of my children, this time I wouldn't be able to. They will remember it as it was.

We always spoke softly to each other. I was attentive to everyone's needs, neglecting my own because I wanted everyone to be happy and that made me happy enough. It filled my heart. I told him, "I'm your wife, do you remember? What happened to you?" Even then, I didn't completely understand. From our home phone I called to the number that appeared on the cell phone I found in his possessions. I thought we knew everything about each other, that there were no secrets between us. I felt as if I was standing quietly at the train station listening to Enya's Caribbean Blue on my headphones, looked peacefully at the sky and, suddenly, without warning, the train hit me at a speed of two hundred and fifty miles per hour. The impact was so powerful for me that I didn't understand what had happened. "You'll always be my first wife," he said to me coldly. I didn't understand what he was saying because, at the time, I didn't fully know what he was doing. I don't know where I got the strength to mend the rift at that moment, I don't know how I managed to calm the storm. I was very scared, just thinking about what the children would go through. I could have died. I didn't trust him anymore, how could I trust him alone with the children, especially if he brought them to this woman, who was the reason he hurt them and me so much. How difficult it is to raise children, so many worries. Why should they suffer now? Because he is so egotistical and evil. He doesn't deserve them or me at all! At all! I hated him! Hated myself! It was a terrible time. It seemed to me that the woman he went with corrupted him and taught him to smoke something, and he never smoked, and what he smoked affected his brain and caused him to behave in such a cruel way. Otherwise, how could it be explained? The way he yelled at me for no real reason and, even if there was one, he shouldn't be yelling at me. The way he tried to make me think that everything was my fault. That I was the reason he was leaving, that I was no good, accusing me for his actions.

I felt like I ruined my children's lives. That it was entirely my fault. How hard it was for me. I didn't want to go back with him to places where we had previously quarreled, or he had made a sour face, or just made us feel like we had to do something to please him in order for him to stay. It would have been good if he had left without paying the price for his mistakes, but that was not the case. He stayed. So I had to stay with him just so my children would be safe with me, so I could protect them. I hated him for his dishonesty and for the fact that the children and I weren't good enough for him. That he didn't love us enough to stop seeking temptation. Why did he go after another woman at all? We got married out of choice. We wanted to be together. From the moment we met, he never left me alone for a day. It was very stifling at first because I was very independent and he wanted to come everywhere with me. Everything we did together turned out very well, he consulted me on everything, even though I told him it was perfectly fine with me if he chose on his own. I wanted to bolster his self-confidence to make his own choices. But he insisted. Over time, I appreciated his desire to consult with me because it made me feel that my opinion was very important to him and maybe, just as I give space to his feelings so that we can be equal, he was doing it back. A relationship of dominance and submissiveness is a failed relationship. It leads nowhere and does not allow people to reach their full potential, not even for those who dominate. They just don't see it. How naive I was. He didn't want to take responsibility for anything. That's why he consulted me on everything so that, if there was a problem, he would have someone to blame. I didn't understand a thing. I didn't interpret even one thing correctly.

I rationalized to myself so I'd be able to tolerate him and stay with him. I explained his behavior as a deprivation he had from high school. He felt rejected by the girls and now he needed to prove something to himself. That is why he lost weight, started working out and wanted to develop his muscles. What a fool! It's not what made him unlikable in high school – his rugged personality was the reason. It all depends on what your personality inside radiates to the outside world. His radiated nothing but bitterness resulting from rude thinking, misinterpretation, wrong conclusions. From what he inferred about himself, mainly from his misinterpretation of the behavior of his surroundings towards him. I had to make excuses for him to myself, or I couldn't bear being in the same room with him or listening to him, talk with him, look at him, at him and his treachery.

Well, if that's really what he wanted, to replace us with an older woman with her own children who, apparently, from the messages I read on this nightmarish phone, he managed to devote himself while humiliating ours. If he couldn't find time for our children, then he should have left us, be of help when needed, to love our children and not to forget or replace them. I would have said good-bye to him with understanding and love, with a broken heart, and we might even remain friends.

I looked at myself in the mirror for a few more minutes, again asking myself, what did I do wrong? What did I do wrong? I think about it again. I didn't deny him anything, I always supported and encouraged him on the simplest things, even after he disappointed me as a friend and partner. Like when I was cold at the cinema and he asked why didn't I bring a jacket – he didn't warm or hug me. Or when I wanted to hold hands with him and he said it was uncomfortable. Or the unpleasant things, like always sleeping with his back to me. And the hardest one, when my dear mother died. Although he knew I was the youngest daughter and knew how attached I was to her, he wasn't a source of comfort and didn't lend a shoulder when I heard about her death. He just sighed impatiently. I explained to myself that his mother also passed away six months ago and it was also hard for him, that's the way I eased my mind. However, that wasn't it. What could I've done at the time? Destroy the only home Nell ever knew and felt safe in just because it wasn't good for me? Neil was only a year old, he wouldn't remember. How long can you wait, believe in a person and excuse his behavior by saying it comes from a good place? That these are inhibitions that, given time, he will be able to overcome. I believed that he had a beautiful soul, it was just hidden by many walls and the inferiority complex that made him half-human/half-monster. I saw a monster in those days. Not a person. A monster. I forced myself to think that maybe he was like that because of the difficulties he was experiencing. I didn't want to judge, I wanted to be a true friend who strengthened, supported and believed in him.

Maybe there is something wrong with me – how long have I waited? 15 years? I should have called it off when he started treating me badly. Before that, he wasn't perfect either, but his voice was soft, he would kiss me at every opportunity, or just touch my hands or back with his hand when we were walking with Nelly when she was a baby. In general, everything changed after the children were born. I was alone. He no longer came home from work at five-thirty to go for a walk. He would arrive at eight, after their showers, first just with Nell and then with both of them; he explained that there is a lot of traffic at five o'clock and it was better for him to wait until it was over. He said it was a waste of money on gas, and that the traffic tired him out. As far as I'm concerned, as long as he was happy, I was happy. In any case, I wanted to take care of my children, I was happy that I gave birth to them safely and that they were healthy. I wanted to be with them. It would have been nice to take a walk together with the children in the stroller in the afternoon and shower them together. Mr. B. suggested we travel together, but only if it was out of town. I am more calm and peaceful than he is. He always needs change and attention.

I sat on the edge of the bed; with elbows on my knees and my face in my palms. He wanted joint custody, to separate the children from me despite knowing how much I cared for the children and how important it was to me that they have stability in their lives. And I want nothing but good for them. Every time they had a vaccination, I would sit by them, all of me cramped, worried about side effects, praying that everything would pass peacefully, strictly following all the instructions, with extreme precision, so that everything would be all right and that these dear children, that I brought into this world, who are my responsibility, would not suffer in any way from wrongdoing on my part. I wanted everything to be good for the children, Mr. B. and me.

Why wasn't he on board? I never thought he was stupid. If not for us, who would our dear children have? Who could they trust more than us? Who could love them more than we do? We gave them life, we are responsible for them. It was our choice to give birth to them, not theirs, and it is our obligation to take care of them always, especially at this age when they are defenseless. It's all so basic, as natural as breathing. We want them to be well, for us to be well, because when they're well, so are we; a wonderful magic circle. May it only be good.

Only good. Only good. What's wrong with that?

"Are you okay?" I heard Ben's deep, beautiful voice.

I got up quickly, with my back to Ben and said quietly, "Yes, just a moment, something got into my eyes. I'll wash my face." I went to the bathroom in my room.

Ben stood quietly, attentively. Even though it was quiet, I felt he was with me, understanding more than I intended to reveal; he was standing there waiting for me to finish. When I came back to the room, through the little moonlight from the window I noticed Ben's strong features. As beautiful and powerful as the personality he radiates, even though he tries hard to hide it. He stood firm and, with a little light, you could see Ben's penetrating and guarding gaze as if confirming that he was here if I needed, not going anywhere and I had no reason to worry, nothing bad would happen to me because he was watching over me, my soul, all of me. I had that feeling each time I was near him.

I approached and said with a smile, "Are you coming? There's no party without the guest of honor, right?", walking past Ben, who was now leaning with one shoulder on the door frame, his hands in his pockets, his gaze following me. My shoulder rubbed against his as I stepped out through the opening.

I kept walking and Ben followed me; suddenly he grabbed my hand warmly and asked, "You can tell me. I won't judge. You can trust me. What are you hiding?" He was very direct.

"Nothing to tell," I replied. What did I have to tell? My troubles? That my husband went with another woman. The way he left me, so rudely. The way he treated me so mercilessly. For no reason? The way he ended a 15-year relationship of friendship, marriage, parenthood, without respect? To me? To the children? To the vows we had made? To our journey together? What is there to tell? I have nothing to tell.

"I can feel you," he said assertively.

I couldn't breathe.

Those words! Did the universe send Ben? How can that even be? Those words! I stood still with my head bowed, afraid that if I looked at him he'd see how I felt about him. He will see how much I appreciated him for this single sentence, what feelings he evoked in me. Suddenly, all the fire within me was extinguished. Although I can sense him – from the moment he signed the contract, and everything I have felt since then, turned out to be true about him, since we share one roof and he is wonderful, really wonderful, but maybe I am making a mistake again. I don't know him at all, maybe he cheated on his wife too; maybe he's a cheater too. Why would my intuitions be any more correct now than before, when they were for Mr. B.? I pulled my hand away from him, gently removing his hand from mine with my other hand. I hurried to keep walking and everything seemed blurry for a moment. I tripped and fell.

When I woke up the next morning, I don't know why, but I opened my computer and read the news on the home page. Since the beginning of the summer vacation, a month ago, I've avoided doing this daily ritual I used to do at home. I'll just update myself a with news around the world and at home. I decided that, on this vacation, I would take a break from life as I knew it, with all its problems. I wanted to connect to myself, to the harmony within.

To feel the beauty and goodness of simplicity again, the peace of mind, to get as far away as possible from this crazy race that Mr. B. dragged us into. The race after progress, out of greed and constant dissatisfaction with what there is; from betrayal to quarrels.

I looked and looked again; I read the news and couldn't believe what I was reading. Main heading:

The lands in the country belong to the residents, no taxes will be paid on the land, the price of a house will be determined according to materials plus labor in all parts of the country. Each title was better than the last. Another title said the minimum wage would triple; another headline said that our taxes had bought the prime minister a vehicle for a sum of $1 million. Great, what do I care? The main thing is that we can get rid of the mortgage. From now on, it will be possible for us to travel abroad every summer. Each time a different destination. Wow, wow. So good.

It's great that people finally understood that if we take care of the welfare of each and every person, then everyone is happy. A happy person is one who minds his own business and doesn't interfere in the business of others. This is good for you, I chuckled for a moment. We don't have to wait for anyone, we are our own saviors. Everyone is good and the world is good. People fix themselves and the world is being fixed. It's good that something has already been fixed. Instead of waiting for a superhero so we don't have to take responsibility, to have someone to blame. It's a good thing we got sober.

"Sil?"

"Mr. B.?" I was surprised, he should be in Italy.

"I love you, Sil, so much! I am sorry for my behavior over the years, and mostly in the last two years. You're my wife. You are dear to me; you and the children are dearest to me. I love you very much. You are so precious to me. Will you forgive me?"

"Do you regret everything you did to me? To us?" I asked in wonder.

"Yes" he said.

"I was your friend every step of the way and you hurt me, through no fault of my own," I continued.

"I know, and I sincerely regret it."

"Do you understand how much it hurt me when I read that letter on your computer desktop? The letter you wrote to her, instead of loving me, courting me, strengthening me and caring for me – you did it for another woman?"

"Let's turn over a new leaf. I will learn from all my mistakes so as never to repeat them. You are my home, you and our children, you are my home, and I love you all so much."

Mr. B. embraced me tightly to him and I embraced him back.

His remorse and appreciation for us surprised me greatly; I was not prepared for this situation. I didn't have time to think, to reflect on things. What he said made me appreciate him, for the courage I never thought he had, to take responsibility after all we've been through, a forgotten sense of love that overwhelmed me. With these words he can turn it all around; the problem is, only time will tell.

Suddenly I heard Neil calling in the background, "Mom, Mom," but I couldn't tear myself away from Mr. B. nor the possibility of a mended reality and the hope that maybe, just maybe, now everything would be better. But the longer Neil's cries continued, the clearer his voice became, and I wasn't sure why his voice sounded worried and scared. Then I also heard Nell crying and saying in a weak voice, "Mom, Mom, wake up!" but I'm awake, I thought to myself. What happened? Why are they sad? Again I heard "Mommy, wake up please!"

"See? Here, I'm awake!" I said, confused. Maybe not?

"Neil, Mom moved her head," I heard Nelly's trembling voice.

"Mom, Mom!" she kept calling loudly.

"Nell? Neil?" I opened my eyes.

"Mommy!" cried Nell, laying down on top of me.

"Mommy!" said Neil after her, and he lay down next to me as well. They were both crying. "Don't cry, don't cry," I said, hurrying to calm them down. "Here, I'm here, I'm fine. See? We're together, everything's fine." It didn't help, they kept hugging me and continued to cry.

Everything still blurry, I saw Nadav, Ari and Ben and they all looked worried; however, they also seemed relieved. They looked tired, smiling hesitantly at me. They stood close to the bed I was on and, with my shaky, weak hands, I hugged my two precious souls.

"What happened?" I asked in a weak, very weak voice.

"You fainted yesterday when you went down the stairs and stumbled. It's good that Ben was able to stop the fall," Ari said.

"But don't worry," he immediately added to calm Nelly, Neil and me down. "You're perfectly fine, especially now that you've opened your eyes," he seemed to want to calm himself, Nadav, and Ben, who were so worried about me.

"Isn't that right, doctor...?" asked Nadav, the doctor standing on the other side of the bed, "Yes. Undoubtedly. Mom woke up, kids, now everything is fine. I need you guys to get up just for a few minutes so I can check on Mom? All right?" said Dr. Bale, his voice soft and sensitive. Ari, Nadav, and Ben came over to help Nell and Neil up. As I watched them take the kids and put their arms around them, I thought, *Can't I be totally okay when I see them like that?!*

The doctor checked, helped me to sit up, and explained that they ran all the necessary tests while I slept and they came out normal. There was a little concern when the pulse was irregular but, towards morning, it was back to normal and it seems that everything is fine now. "You have to stay with us a while longer and, if everything goes well, we'll let you go," he said, writing, "Maybe even today," he finally added.

"Thank you," I said. I hadn't even noticed that I was in a hospital room.

I spread my arms out to my children and smiled. They came to me, Nelly still crying and Neil too, Ari, Nadav and Ben came in closer and everyone created a circle around me, a circle that lent a sense of security and love. They caressed the children's backs in soothing movements.

"Thank you," I told them, and tears welled up in my eyes. I couldn't stop them.

"Thank you so much for everything!" I said, looking at Ari and Nadav. It was hard for me to look at Ben. I looked at Ben for a moment, smiled and immediately looked down.

"You're so great. You are irreplaceable," I said softly.

Nelly and Neil lay beside me, their heads on my chest, and I stroked their hair.

I recovered quickly. I don't like hospitals. I wanted to go home as soon as possible. I didn't want to disrupt our wonderful summer vacation with illness or hospitals. I wanted to go back to us all being healthy and joyful.

Nell and Neil were both born by cesarean section and, in both cases, I helped myself recover quickly to get out of the hospital and back home. Now I couldn't wait to get back to the house on the beach that became a home and, in such a short period of time, a safe haven.

During my pregnancy with Nell I developed gestational diabetes. She came out big – just over nine pounds. The C-section was scheduled for Monday morning at eight o'clock and I was supposed to be the first, so I spent Sunday night in the hospital during which contractions started. I didn't know at the time that they were contractions; after all, it was my first birth. Around six o'clock in the morning, however, they got stronger, so I informed the nurse that I thought I had contractions. Indifferently and skeptically, the nurse connected me to the monitor and, when she came back after a few minutes to check, the apathy disappeared from her face. Just before rushing out of the room, she said the contractions were two minutes apart.

The nurse came back quickly, this time with a doctor and a wheelchair. They took me to the room I stayed in the night before. The doctor wanted to check the opening. I said, "What for? You don't have to! I'm having a c-section." I didn't want her to check. Why hurt me if I'm not having a normal birth anyway? I'd learned a little bit from the prenatal book I bought.

The doctor insisted, gently but assertively, waiting for the contraction to pass, then she pushed her hand in and said I had an opening of five centimeters, took out her hand and, with it, my water broke.

They sat me back down in the wheelchair and rushed me to the delivery room. On the way, Helen, a sweet obstetrician, suggested that I have a normal birth, but I had read in a prenatal book that a baby born to a diabetic mother in a vaginal birth can be born with a malformation if you pull his hand incorrectly. The sensitivity is greater than a child born to a non-diabetic mother, so I immediately refused and explained why: "No. I am diabetic. The baby can be injured during childbirth." She probably didn't need the detailed explanation. She already understood in 'diabetic,' being a doctor, after all. She let me finish out of politeness, perhaps out of compassion, because I found the strength to explain, despite the pain of the contractions. We arrived at the operating room and, so it was, that at seven-fifty on the morning of October 31, 2000, I saw my dear Nelly for the first time.

For Neil's birth, I was afraid to try a vaginal birth after the cesarean. Mr. B. remembered that the doctor who suggested a cesarean birth for Nelly said that the next births would have to be cesarean as well, that the risk was higher for the mother to have a vaginal birth after a cesarean birth. A very low percentage, but still, I was afraid to leave my Nelly and my sweet newborn son alone, without a mother. I insisted on giving birth to him by c-section as well. From now on, it's no longer just me I have to take care of. The courage that had accompanied me my whole life gave way to the fear that came with responsibility, and it has stayed since the kids were born and will probably always remain.

Neil was so comfortable in the womb, he had no intention of coming out early. The c-section was scheduled for nine o'clock, but was performed at twelve fifty, as urgent cases from the delivery room preceded us in the operating room. As Neil was seemingly taken out against his will, every night as soon as it got dark he would fall asleep.

On the third day of being in hospital, I insisted I be released in order to get back home to Nelly so she wouldn't feel my absence for too long.

Anyway, today I was discharged from the hospital at 11:00 a.m. and we drove back to the beach house.

Nadav came over to pick me up, he didn't want me to climb the stairs. "Thank you, I can do it alone." I insisted.

We went up to my room. On the way up I said, "It was a great party. You don't know how much I appreciate it. I'm sorry I ruined it."

"You didn't ruin anything. even without you it was a great party," Nadav said.

I laughed. Such a good soul, this Nadav!

"Besides, we've already thought about how you could make it up to us. A movie. What movie did you want, kids?" asked Ari.

"The Sorcerer's Apprentice," Nell said.

"Yes. That's it! So you have until tomorrow night to recover because we're going out to the movies," Ari said.

"I think no matter how hard I try, I can't thank you enough. I love you all very much."

"No more than we love you," Ari said, smiling.

"That's the best thanks there is," Nadav said.

I sat down on the bed. Ari suggested that everyone go downstairs to let me get ready and, in the meantime, they would load super tasty ice cream onto waffle cones.

I immediately said there was no need. I'm fine. No need to bother. Nevertheless, the kids were so happy and wanted to make one for me that I corrected myself right away and said: "I'd love some vanilla ice cream. Thank you."

They all went downstairs, except for Ben who stayed.

"Are you coming?" Nadav asked Ben.

"Yes, in a minute," Ben replied.

Ben sat down on the eighteenth-century-style armchair. His legs spread apart, his elbows on his legs, his fingers intertwined.

Ben looked me straight in the eye and said, "Tell me? What happened? I want to know," he insisted.

"Nothing happened," I replied, "I haven't thanked you yet. Thank you, without you…"

"I won't leave until you tell me what happened," he interrupted. "I'll wait here until you're ready to tell me. You have to get it off your chest, whatever it is."

I was silent and looked down. I really wanted to tell him. For a while now I have wanted a male's opinion on everything that happened. I felt very close to Nadav and Ari and I wanted to ask them more than once, without revealing the identities of the people in the story, but I couldn't. I was ashamed. What if they understood it was me? They are sharp. What would they think of me? What will Ben think of me…?

After a few minutes of silence, I said, "I don't know where to start." Ben's face was tense and his palms were now clenched, as if he was ready to punch someone.

He sat there and waited.

I started from the end and recounted the entire ordeal. Finally I said, "I waited for him but he didn't wait for me, in many ways, some of which I prefer to keep to myself." I was ashamed to say them out loud.

I finished talking and thought to myself that I must have hit my head really hard if, when I lost consciousness, I lost all connection with reality and thought Mr. B. had come and apologized. He even took responsibility. The blow had to be strong.

It would have behooved Mr. B. to listen more carefully in literature class; he would have understood, like Antigone, where his pride would lead him. Barricading himself in his insistence that he's right. Those characters in the play at least had high morals and acted in their name. In whose name does he act? In his own? Ridiculous, he's no hero, certainly not a tragic one. He creates problems just so there will be problems. Maybe he had a need to conform to society, so if everyone has problems at home, why shouldn't we?

"A man who chooses to marry the woman he loves, builds a home with her and starts a family shouldn't be able to see himself without his family. It's not just about him anymore. He's part of something larger that he must protect. He should appreciate what he's built and what he has, because he feels and knows that he has nothing more precious than that." Ben said in a decisive voice, trying to find the right words, to construct the sentences correctly so that the meaning of what he wanted to express would come out as clearly as it was for him in his mind.

Ben was direct, he didn't beat around the bush: "He didn't feel enough responsibility for you, to keep you safe and not hurt you. Why did you stay with him?"

Because I am not like him, I couldn't truly understand what his problem was. I could never do such things to him, so that's why I couldn't perceive what he was doing to me.

I finally said, "I was scared."

"What were you afraid of? You seem to be doing just fine on your own," Ben continued to ask and fortify me.

"Even then, I was fine on my own. Everything was hard for him to do, he was always sighing. I rarely asked him to take the dog out, even after a sleepless night when Nelly or Neil was sick. There were times when I wanted us to do it together, even before the children were born, to walk together with Pinch, in the evening. Just to be together. It's nice, isn't it? He would sigh and there would be a million excuses. I would always take the dog out for a walk on my own. Taking out the garbage? He thought first about whether his car was in front or on the side because, if it was in the front, then he would have to go down to the garbage room from the back and go back and forth; it's a detour, instead of going straight down the front to the car. So many considerations for such a simple and routine thing."

"So why?" he asked.

"I don't know why. I'm a person who sees goals and, sometimes, the end justifies the means."

"Pinch?"

"We said goodbye to Pinch when Neil was four and Nelly was seven. I adopted her when I was 20 years old and she accompanied Nelly and Neil since they were born with great devotion and love. She only knew how to be devoted and loving, our Pinch. She was also black, but bigger than Anch, a mixed Shepard and Retriever. It was very difficult for me, for us, to say goodbye to her. Neil and Nell we so young and the separation was very difficult. She was a blessing and she was so loved! Even now, it hurts to remember," I wiped away tears.

Ben looked at me. His gaze made me feel appreciated, maybe even admired. He didn't have to say anything to make me feel that way.

I smiled and looked out at the sky again as if hoping that, from there, I would draw the strength and wisdom to find the right words to explain to myself what had happened.

I continued to explain in a quiet voice, while thinking, so that I too would understand:

"At first I acted out of confusion. When everything exploded, I didn't understand what happened. When I discovered the betrayal, he denied it and started blaming me for things so I would think I was the reason for him leaving. I blamed myself because I'm inclined to first check myself before checking others.

"In the second stage, not that there were stages, but that's the order things happened," I said, stuttering a little, "I acted out of fear. I believe in reward and punishment so I thought I must have done something wrong and I need to correct it because, otherwise, it wouldn't have happened to me. Then I was more scared when I heard the words 'joint custody' and I didn't agree to it. I knew what the consequences would be. In general, if he has chosen to love himself and only himself, and doesn't consider those around him, it doesn't mean that he has the right to hurt others and destroy the good in them. To hurt me and our dear children just for the needs of an irresponsible 16-year-old? Although, I can tell you that there are responsible 16-year-olds who could teach him something about responsibility.

"In the end, I stayed with him because I said to myself that everyone make mistakes; he still doesn't understand how wrong he was and who knows what awaits him outside once he leaves the safe life with us, so I will help him stay and, one day, he will be glad he didn't leave. I was especially happy that the joint custody issue was taken off the table.

"I hated him and wanted him gone, but I thought that if this madness ever happened to me, I would want him to be strong for me and not let me go. For him to remember the good things about me, the reasons he married me in the first place, and hold on tightly to them so that they would give him strength not to give up on me.

"Still confused by everything, even now," I added softly.

I lowered my head and crumpled the blanket in my hands. I didn't know how to bear it, I felt like I didn't deserve it! Everything that happened to me. I held back from crying, I held back, but the tears, the tears didn't listen to me. He didn't appreciated anything! The children are also mine; I didn't need him to appreciate me for taking care of them, but everything else, everything I hoped for him, everything he wanted, all the support. It hurt me as if I was the enemy, not the woman he has shared his life with since he was 22.

"I thought to myself that if he just apologies and admitted that he made a mistake, everything would look different. I would surely forgive him, appreciated him for owning up to it. We all make mistakes and we all want to be forgiven and if he thinks he wasn't wrong then he maybe go, he shouldn't stay, it would be better that way. He doesn't love me or the children. Those who love do not behave this way. A life without love is not a life. And if Mr. B. wanted to return without taking responsibility for his mistakes, how could I live with that?? I couldn't! I couldn't! So things didn't go back to normal, they just hung somewhere between earth and heaven. In limbo. It was an impossible situation."

Ben stood up and came to me. He took both of my hands. I didn't look up, I couldn't. Yes, I could feel Ben's compassionate, his protective gaze, I could even feel the anger inside him.

"Be careful, sweetie, don't fall, look at the stairs, not the ice cream," I heard Ari tell Neil. "Better the ice cream fall than you."

"Where's Ben? Why didn't he come?" I heard Neil ask Ari.

"Never mind, we brought him a bowl with vanilla and chocolate ice cream. We decided he looked like a vanilla and chocolate person, right?" said Ari to Neil.

I took my hands away and wiped my tears, saying, "I'm sorry."

"Don't be sorry, love," Ben said.

In my heart, I smiled for a split second when I heard Ben say those words; I didn't expect him to speak to me that way.

I wiped my tears away, no need to bring everyone down; it's heavy enough for me, I don't want to burden the children. If it will be difficult for them, it will not be easy for me either; on the contrary, it will be even harder for me.

Nell brought me the bowl with the vanilla ice cream. Such wonderful children. They knew I'd prefer the ice cream in the bowl, without a waffle cone.

"Oh, yummy," I said. I didn't feel like eating anything at all. I took the ice cream from Nelly and placed it on the bedside table. "You know, kids? I completely forgot about the treasure hunt I made for you."

I got up to get the first note. My body was still weak and sore, but I stood up as if my strength had completely returned to me. "Here it is. The first note." I gave it to Nelly.

"May I join the hunt?" asked Nadav.

"Sure you can." Neil replied.

I felt that I fully recovered. I smiled and took a deep breath.

"Thank you, Mom," Nelly said, hugging me.

"You're welcome, my beloved girl." I hugged her tightly to me.

After the ice cream, everyone followed the clues.

Ben reached the door of the room, turned around and said, "The way I see it, you each got married for different reasons. You married a selfish person who caused problems. You accepted his behavior because you vowed to love him, for better or worse. Let's say I understand that, but now? Why now? When he's lost that right? Don't you think he has forfeited the right to receive anything from you? Moreover, you don't owe him anything. Marriage is a covenant between two people and he broke that covenant," he stated. "Why are you still committed to it?"

"You're right. I could put up with it because I hoped that one day it would change and, if not, then there were other good things I could see in him and they made up for the bad. But now that he's broken our trust, I don't have the will or the strength to contain his egoism anymore; I also had expectations in life," I said as I tried to overcome the sadness he could hear in my voice. To live alongside a person who is happy with his lot, loving and giving, no matter what happens, we would be able to face it together. And for each other. And, if necessary, against the entire world. I didn't think my husband would be so messed up, without any emotion or soul. Just an empty vessel.

"It's a pity. I thought there was a lot more to him. I thought he was a good soul and I just needed to understand the source of his struggles in order to help him break free and be happy, as he deserves. Sometimes I came to the conclusion that what was holding him back were his fears, preventing him from giving of himself completely. I never saw this coming. How did he not see how great he had it? He didn't understand that being happy with his lot, ironic as it may have sounded, would have helped him grow and succeed beyond anything he could have imagined. He often seemed disgruntled. It's great that there are aspirations, and an end can justify the means, but only if the end itself is just.

"When I think of you and your wonderful children, I can't understand how he wasn't already satisfied. People like him will never be satisfied even if they get everything they want. The problem wasn't you or the kids. It was him," Ben said.

Thank you, universe, for sending Ben to me, to help me.

I heard the children running up the stairs, "We found it! Mom, we found it!"

"I don't know him, but I do know you," Ben continued.

He knows me? Then it wasn't just me, feeling that he was with me every time we were in the same room. And all along I thought he didn't see me at all.

"You're a person that makes life look easier than it is, you radiate confidence, you're a wonderful mother, you instill a feeling of belonging to those around you, your intentions are always good, you're a good soul. He had to be blind not to see it. I apologize in advance for what I'm about to say: He's not blind. I think he had to find bad things in you so as not to feel bad about himself." He paused for a moment then added, "He didn't want to feel like he lost something others could only dream of."

"I'm so ashamed of what happened to me that I haven't even told my closest friends." The children's voices were close now. "I don't want my children to know about anything I've told you. Thank you. Thank you so much for the conversation and thank you for the support, thank you for everything," I said, again trying to hold back tears.

"You're welcome," he said in a deep voice, "I'm here for you. Whenever you want. For whatever you need."

One of Ben's hands was clenched into a fist; I got the impression he was thinking of Mr. B.

"We found it, Mom!" the children called, excited and out of breath from running up the stairs. As they entered the room, they said together, "Thank you, Mom. The box is very beautiful and the notepad you put in it is also very beautiful," Nelly said.

"Thank you, Mom," Neil said.

"The box is empty now. You will fill it with all the beautiful experiences you will have. Every time you have a good and happy experience, write it down on one of the pages in the notepad and put it in the box; don't forget to write the date so, one day, when you're older, you can open the box and remember all the good experiences you had, written in your handwriting. That way you will always know who you are. These notes will be priceless, worth more than anything. And, one day, far, far into the future... you too, like me now, will be able to sit with your children and share all the wonderful memories you've kept in the box."

"I know what I want to write already," Nelly said, happily.

"I don't know how to write yet," Neil said a little disappointed.

"I'll write for you until you learn how to write and then you'll continue on your own. Okay? In the meantime, I thought you could make drawings. You love to draw."

"Okay," said Neil, still a little disappointed that he couldn't keep up with his sister. He wants to be as good as she is in everything and I couldn't be more satisfied; she's the best role model there could be.

CHAPTER 6

08.02.2010

*W*hen I got out of bed today, my body still hurt, but I felt immense relief. I felt that I had new and very strong powers. For a long time, I didn't want things for myself. Now I want to buy myself a new outfit and let my hair out. I often go with my hair pulled back, tied tightly in a ponytail. Today I feel like letting it loose. I put on a white summer dress and go barefoot with Anch for my morning walk. It was almost seven o'clock. I quietly left the room and pulled back the cream-colored curtains, embossed with small white flowers and leaves, so that Nell and Neil, who'd fallen asleep with me last night right after we finished reading Cinderella together, wouldn't wake up so early. After all, we are on a vacation. Everyone was asleep when I went out with Anch, At least, that's what I thought. I didn't check the other rooms but it was very quiet in the house. With peace of mind, I enjoyed the cool morning breeze and the seashore. The sound of the waves rushing to the sand was pleasant, calming, healing all wounds.

I'll prepare an Asian dish for today's meal, I thought to myself as I walked. Stir-fry and sushi. I love sushi with carrots and avocados. Nelly does to. For Neil, I'll make it with scallion and cucumber. Nelly also likes that combination. I'll check if I have a ripe avocado, at least one; one is enough; even half is enough. Not too soft, though. For dessert, I'll make apple strudel. Before everyone wakes up, I'll make blintzes with a sweet soft cheese, vanilla and cinnamon, and some with chocolate. Nelly loves both, especially chocolate. Neil will prefer only chocolate and I like the vanilla and cinnamon. I wonder what the others will like.

The boys would probably prefer the ones with the sweet cheese, vanilla and cinnamon.

It turned out I was wrong. Nadav loved chocolate; Ari had no preference and Ben wanted only cheese. He was satisfied with only one. I don't know why, but it seems to me that Ben keeps a lot of secrets in his heart, many more than I keep in mine.

In the evening we all went to the movies, but without Ben. He couldn't join us.

The 'Sorcerer's Apprentice' was very enjoyable. Nicolas Cage was at his best and Nelly fell in love with him. "What other movies is he in?" she asked, and the only one I could recall at that moment was 'The Rock.'

"Excellent movie! There's a part that explains how wars begin; how fear and misunderstanding can lead to war, and how it could be that people who don't even know each other, who otherwise would have been friends, can kill each other," I explained to Nelly.

"You mean the shower scene?" asked Nadav.

"Yes," I said, surprised.

"I thought about it too when I saw the movie," Nadav said.

"What are you talking about?" Ari joined the conversation after Neil was talking with him about Dave from the movie.

"About the movie 'The Rock,'" Nadav said.

"Great movie," Ari said, "One of the best."

"Right? Excellent movie! We have it. If you want to watch it again..."

"There are some scenes that are too hard for children..." said Ari.

"I'm censoring," I said, smiling. I really do censor.

The children wanted to sleep next to me tonight too. Ben came up to say goodnight and ask how the movie was. The children shared more than Ben intended to hear, I think, but he was very patient and pleasant, he showed interest in a soft voice, he was very attentive and he especially handled Anch very well, who was non-stop jumping and excited. Ben's appearance is tough, but he has a very sensitive soul, well hidden behind walls. He's hiding something, I'm sure of it. It takes one to know one.

I don't have to understand it, just accept it. That's what he needs.

"Why didn't you join us?" I asked.

"I couldn't," he said, his gaze agonizing. "I'm sorry," Ben apologized.

"There's no reason," I answered quickly, "just for you to also have fun."

"I'm glad you enjoyed it," he said and smiled seriously.

"Good night, kids," he said.

"Good night, Ben," Neil said.

"Good night, Ben," Nelly said.

I escorted Ben to the doorway "Thank you. Good night."

"You're welcome, good night." he said, smiling, his hands in his pockets jeans and a black T-shirt that fit him well. Ben already started to go down the stairs; he turned around and said good night again.

"Good night." I replied, smiling, and went back into the room.

"What book should we read tonight? What did you choose?" I asked as I got into bed between Nelly and Neil. Anch jumped on us making tiger sounds. It happens sometimes. Not the fact that she jumps on us, that happens all the time, rather the sounds of the tiger. Our Anch has a need to prove that great powers lie within her, she knows that her small appearance is misleading.

"I want the story 'No Place Like Home,'" Neil said.

"I want 'Hanna's Sabbath Dress,'" said Nelly.

"You both chose great books, we'll read them both. Which shall we start with?" I asked.

"Mine," Neil said.

"I don't care," Nelly said.

It really doesn't matter to her. She's so easy-going.

"I don't care either," Neil said.

"So let's start with 'Hanna's Sabbath Dress' then" I said.

Neil made a sound of, 'What? We don't start with mine?' and gave me the book he brought. "That's impolite," I said, "Be generous and kind."

"Well, fine, Hanna then," he said.

"You're a wonderful boy," I said and kissed him. "You didn't lose, you showed us how wonderful and strong you are." Nelly seemed satisfied.

I read 'Hanna's Sabbath Dress' and suddenly something dawned on me. I explained to Nelly and Neil that, while we respect and help others, you should never go with stranger to a secluded place. If you are in a crowded place then it's okay to help. I never thought of it that way. As a child I also loved this story very much, especially when Hanna said that she did not regret helping the man, but also didn't want to disappoint her mother by dirtying the dress her mother sewed for her.

After watching too many police investigation programs on TV and, especially after having children, I've learned to examined things more carefully. And even though I'm often ridiculed by associates, family, and friends, I persist, preferring to be safe rather than sorry. I've read this story to the children before, but never really dwelt on it. I focused on the fact that Hannah didn't regret helping the man, even though it soiled the dress she loved so much. I wanted them to take away from this story that a good deed doesn't leave black spots, rather it offers many points of light. Wishing it very much for myself, wishing it would happen already.

We also read 'No Place Like Home' and we felt like Mole; although our house is small, there is nothing like home. We missed our home and, without realizing it, idealized the life we had. However, we did not regret for a moment staying at the beach house. We were having a great time and felt very comfortable here. We missed Mr. B. very much, or at least the man we knew before all the quarrelling over the last two years, although we didn't say it explicitly. The way we loved watching cartoons together at the cinema, the walks, the yogurt ice creams, the nonsense we used to say and, in general, the times together.

Suddenly I clung to more distant memories. "Neil?" I said. "Do you know how long Nelly waited for you?" I said, hugging them both to me. Anch already fell asleep on the books, so there was no one to come between us. "When Nelly was two-and-a-half years old, she used to ask, 'when will I have a brother or sister? I want a brother or sister.'" Neil smiled and so did Nelly.

"When you were in my belly, we asked Nelly: 'What do you want to have? A brother or sister?' And Nelly said a brother and, at the next visit to the doctor we found out that Nelly would have a brother." I hugged them harder and they both laid their heads on me.

"When you were born, Neil, Nelly asked me one day, 'Mom, when is he going to play with me and talk to me?' I explained to Nelly that you were still little and, in a little while, when you grow up a bit, you'll talk to her and play with her. Every toy Nelly had, she gave you, played with you, waiting patiently until you grew up and could play with her. More than once, she gave up her toys for you because you were young and you didn't understand. She did it willingly and lovingly. And you? Growing up, every time you took something from the fridge you would share it with Nell. When you went shopping with me when Nell was at school, you would take two of anything you wanted for yourself so that would she received the same, you know?" I felt them both satisfied and at peace. Their recent competitiveness, Nell wanting to maintain her advantage in the age difference and Neil wanting to be like her, was unnecessary in my opinion; it was violating the harmony. It's very important to me to ensure that their friendship, their bond, be strong, that they always be each other's best friends and enjoy being together.

We heard the Skype ringing. "Dad! Mom, Daddy is calling," Nelly said, sounding happy and excited. Neil was happy too, and they both ran to the computer to answer. I was excited too, all these memories that I had forgotten about flooding back to me.

Mr. B. wanted to see me and talk to me and asked why I didn't answer yesterday. He tried many times and, even today, he tried many times, so what happened? Nelly recounted the events from yesterday, Neil filled in the missing pieces, and Mr. B. was very concerned, asking if I was okay now. It was good to speak as we used to. It is clear to me today that nothing will be the same as before. Not out of revenge. I used to feel like I was stupid for believing in love and friendship. I don't want to stop feeling that way. Because of his mistakes, I'd lose myself. I do believe in love, I am a hopeless romantic and, one day, I will find someone who thinks as I do. There must be someone who will love and appreciate me, who will enjoy his time with me, without games, lies or deception, who will see the good in me and not be afraid of it, who will understand me. Now he's worrying about me the way he used to. However, during the time he was with her, (let's call it his 'mindless period,' a period without a mind) I had, as it turns out in retrospect, a panic attack. I thought it was a virus, but when I described it to the homeopath and then to the doctor, they both diagnosed it as a panic attack. Mr. B. mocked me for how my body reacted physically. I almost fainted.

I finally came to my senses when I heard him talking to our children, obviously frightened since they'd never even seen me sick and, suddenly, I could barely stand. I called them to me, told them I was fine, and that it would help if they just lay next to me. It really helped. I finally got up, we brushed our teeth and went to bed; luckily, all this happened before bedtime. I slept with them in their room. How terrible the way he treated me! How terrible I felt because I was trapped, and he understood it and took advantage of it. I realized that later. I didn't see a good way out with the children, I couldn't trust him with anything, his judgment, his conscience, his morals. I couldn't trust him. How could I agree to a divorce and shared custody? It was clear to me that I couldn't.

CHAPTER 7

08.10.2010

*T*oday Ari and Nadav are hosting a party. Nelly and Neil are also having friends over – their new friends from one of the houses nearby, and they are having their own party.

I wanted to help Ari and Nadav organize, but they wouldn't let me do anything. I insisted that it wasn't a bother so, in order for me to stop nagging them, they let me arrange the candles. I thought again about 'Hanna's Sabbath Dress' and said to Ari and Nadav, while arranging the candles in the jars, how what was appropriate in the seventies and eighties just isn't today. They said, now that I brought it up, that the story wasn't suitable even then and it should have come with a booklet of warnings.

It was a great party. Nadav and Ari are so talented at this. The party was a success. They have great, pleasant, easy-going friends and I got the impression that they have a healthy attitude towards life.

We played a game of Pantomime: movies, books, shows, proverbs, etc. It was a delightful and entertaining evening, and I'm grateful to the two wonderful friends who insisted I attend the party. They also tried to persuade Ben to join, but without success. After the delicious meal that Nadav and Ari prepared with care and excellence, everyone mingled. They talked about everything that's going on in the country, successes, opportunities and missed ones, mutual friends who have left, mortgages and more.

I thought about all the good people who care about others and want to live in peace, brotherhood, and freedom, as they deserve; activists such as Eleanor Roosevelt and Dr. Martin Luther King, Jr. And people who want to contribute and advance the world like Bill Gates and Elon Musk. All the creators: screenwriters, novelists, musicians, who give the world color, joy and harmony, connecting people. All the wonderful people who care about animals, who raise awareness and how good it would be if all their efforts would bear fruit and this world would really be a better place and no one would suffer or lack anything. In general, that everyone would live with love in their hearts, in peace, wanting good for others as they want for themselves and what they hate for themselves they wouldn't want for others. May we already be wise enough for this to happen.

I thought about how sad it is, heartbreaking, that all those good intentions, all the desire to make the world a better place, with sensitivity and deep understanding, all the sacrifice and efforts still do not yield the desired results.

Everyone raised a toast, each one said what he was grateful for, and it was very nice.

It was my turn and I said, without thinking, "Let's raise a glass to Martin Luther King, Steven Spielberg, Bill Gates, and Elon Musk, who have worked and continue to work to improve the lives of human beings, all life." I intended to continue: PETA, MFA, FOA but the silence in the room caused me to stop. It was very quiet, everyone still with their glass raised, watching. I thought to myself that maybe now was a good time for the earth to open its mouth and swallow me. I must have embarrassed Nadav and Ari in front of their friends. They must be regretting inviting me now. Everyone's faces looked surprised and some had their jaws about to drop, although, after a second of silence, maybe two, that lasted like an eternity to me, they smiled in agreement or maybe they were just being polite, and I smiled in the hope that someone would say something before I evaporated.

"Amen," Nadav said.

CHAPTER 8

08.22.2010

$\mathcal{E}$ ver since I confided in Ben, I've noticed he tends to be around me more often. As long as he was at the house, he stayed close. When I folded the laundry, he paired the matching socks for me though, as careful as I am, one of them always disappears as if the washing machine has its own Bermuda Triangle for socks.

Despite the time that it takes to clean the dishes, pots and pans, I prefer to prepare the food and bake myself rather than buying it ready-made. That way I can adjust it exactly to my taste. I've also noticed that when you prepare your own food, there's an added secret ingredient: the energy of the person who prepares it. That is the reason why the exact same recipe made by two different people who followed the same instructions will never turn out exactly the same. Anyway, many of the times I made food in the kitchen, Ben was there too. Saying something pleasant, bringing a smile to my face, helping by taking things out or putting them back in the fridge, even putting dishes into the dishwasher or emptying it. He didn't shy away from cleaning dishes himself, even when I insisted that he not. I felt that he wanted to take away all the bad memories and create new, wonderful experiences in their place. I felt that he wanted to remove the bad from my life and bring only good into it. He really managed to increase the light to overcome the darkness.

In the afternoon, we had a picnic at the beach. A picnic like in the movies. We brought a checkered tablecloth and a basket filled with delicacies. We spread a white sheet on the sand and put the table-cloth and basket on it. Everything turned out beautifully, the feeling was pleasant but the picture-perfect meal at the beach turned quickly from a movie scene to reality – the wind blew up the sand and it covered all that was on the sheet and in the basket. The picnic was different from the one I planned, but it was an experience and it was a wonderful lesson – next time we'll have the picnic in the living room facing the sea, with the air conditioner on. In general, Nell and Neil have seemed very happy this whole summer. They became very attached to the place as well as the company of the children from the neighboring homes, as if this had always been our life; the scars seemed to have disappeared, as if they had never existed. As for me, I really, really hope that this is indeed the case.

The children and the dog from next door joined the picnic. It was fun. We toyed with all kinds of dreams, such as: If we were to create the world, what would we add to it? We invented a story, built from a collection of parts, each adding their imagination in turn and, after a few amusing and sometimes scary turns, we created an incredibly beautiful story. Afterward, the children all ran to the water.

"Hello, how are you?" asked Ruth, the neighbor who came to pick up the children.

"Fine, thank you," I replied, "and you?" I asked, smiling shyly. Why did I smile shyly? What will be with my self-confidence?

"We're fine too, thank you. We're going to my parents; it's time to take the kids to get ready."

"They've been in the water for almost an hour. They're having a lot of fun together, all of them," I said.

"Yes, you have wonderful children, very mature and polite. My kids love them. Very much. It's a shame you have to leave at the end of the summer," she said. I'll tell Nelly and Neil, it's important to me that they know they're loved.

"Thank you. My children also love your children, and they don't rush to love. They can keep in touch on FaceTime or Skype until we come back here." Ruth agreed. Great. I wanted to keep the good things in their lives, especially this summer.

"I'll go get them out of the water. By the way, have you seen our dog?" asked Ruth.

"No, but I'll help you find him. Maybe he's at our place, he was courting our Anch earlier." We both chuckled.

"Thank you," Ruth said.

"You're welcome," I said, getting up towards the house, "Could you tell Nell and Neil that I'll be right back and to come out of the water too?" I shouted to her as I walked.

"Sure, no problem," Ruth replied.

"Hey Ari, have you seen the neighbor's casted dog, maybe?" I asked.

"Who?"

"The neighbor's dog," I replied, looking for him all over the living room.

"What?" said Ari.

"What?" I said while searching.

"What did you call him?" asked an amused Ari.

"Casted?" I asked, and we both smirked.

"Why?" he asked, again amused.

"Do you know those dogs that run like their body is made of one piece? They look like they've been cast."

"You know? I'm a person who is ever hardly surprised, and you manage to surprise me every time." Ari said.

"Yes," added Nadav, who was in the kitchen preparing pesto sauce, based on the smell. I didn't notice he was there.

"So I understand that no dog came in here," I said.

"Especially not a casted one," Nadav replied.

"I thought he ran in here after Anch," I said, hurrying back to my children.

Later, when evening began to fall, Ari and Nadav's friend arrived. I was in the kitchen, making zucchini pie and sweet kugel without the nuts. It's not easy to squeeze these zucchini, but the result is worth the effort. The children love it very much, too.

All this time, I heard Ari and Nadav's friend talking at quite a volume. About New Year's Eve, a party he threw and how it's a shame they didn't come; criticizing the guests' lives and how the years didn't do them any good; the way they looked. He laughed and talked and laughed and talked, but he was the only one laughing and talking. You've got to give them credit that they were still there with him. Not that I was eavesdropping, but his voice was so loud that even a deaf person could hear what he was saying.

I put the pies away, one in the oven and one in the toaster oven, washed the dishes and went to take Anch for her evening walk until the food was ready. The kids were in the middle of a game on the Wii.

I went downstairs with Anch in her harness and I heard him still giggling, this time about the chubby shape of one of their friends from high school. I don't know what came over me but I couldn't hold back and addressed him:

"Excuse me, it was hard not to overhear what you said – you fasted?"

"And?" he said rudely.

"Most people who fast believe in God. Are you one of the 'most?'" I asked.

"What?" he asked.

"Do you believe in God?" said Ari responding for me, completing me.

"Yes," he answered decisively.

"So how can you criticize his creations?" I asked.

He was silent. It seemed he was searching for an answer, his procrastination indicating that he couldn't find one.

"And, in general," I added, "I don't think it's right to criticize people's appearance. Is there anyone who wouldn't want to be beautiful? Is there anyone who wouldn't want to feel good about themselves? No one chooses to look bad. Weight gain in someone who was once thin is often a sign of a crisis. There are those who are more beautiful when they are not thin, and there are those who have always been that way and feel good about themselves. So why judge? After all, there's only one judge, right?" Honestly, he reminded me of Mr. B., I answered him as I felt like answering Mr. B. Constantly criticizing. Now that I'm writing this, I wonder, maybe the whole point of his criticism stems from his fear of what other people think, of society's criticism, so he strikes first, taking himself out of the picture, out of the possibility of being the one who's picked on, just like Nadav and Ari's friend. In fact, it's about insecurity and nothing more.

He looked at Ari and Nadav, and they smiled as if they wanted to say, "Well? What do you have to say for yourself now? She's right." Again, I felt this pleasant feeling in their company, the support and understanding, the security of togetherness. I've missed it so much for years. It's good my parents equipped me with a of a good dose of self-confidence so that I had reserves for all those years I lacked. Over the past few months, I felt like it was starting to run out.

"Sorry for interfering, sometimes it's hard for me to hold my tongue," I said. I didn't feel like I needed to apologize, but for Ari and Nadav, I did.

"It's perfectly fine. On the contrary, thank you for enlightening that caveman." Ari said.

I went outside.

I turned my head for a moment, checking the time on the big clock on the wall; the pies were in the oven and I should have paid closer attention to the time. The friend was huddling with Ari and Nadav, probably asking if everything was okay with me. Is everything okay with me? I wonder. I think I need to let go of the past, leave everything behind, not allow it to seep into me anymore and change me. I used to be kind, pleasant, smiling, creating a pleasant atmosphere around me, trusting others. But since I found the letter on the computer, I have been making it difficult for everyone around me. I need to find myself again, before it's too late and even I won't be able to stand who I've become.

It was a pleasant evening; the sky was mostly pink as if someone had brushed several shades of pink, light blue and a bit of white. I heard Nell and Neil as I passed by their bedroom window, still playing on the Wii. Nell finally managed to hit a home run. How fun that must be – it's hard to hit a home run. Neil succeeds to hit a few in every single game; we've barely succeeded to hit one in five games and, when that happens, it feels like a real achievement.

Anch ran around freely. I don't think she'll be happy about going back to the apartment in the city now that she has gotten used to the new place, the space she has to herself and the freedom from her leash. She's so different from Pinch. Pinch would come back and bite her collar, playing or wanting me to tie her up so we don't get lost. Pinch looked after all of us, maybe it was her 'wolf' side. Anch only looks after herself.

Funny.

I took a tennis ball with me, I've seen in the movies that people who took their dogs to a walk in the park often threw a ball, and the dog would bring it back them, and so the four-legged friends went for a walk and played. I finally managed to remember to bring a ball with me and it was good that I remembered to use it too on the way back, before the walk was over. I was curious if our Anch would run after the ball and bring it back to me. I followed Anch running after the ball and saw Nadav, waved at him, smiled and hoped that he was coming in peace, and that my earlier words had not disrupted the harmony of this summer.

"He who guards his mouth and his tongue keeps his soul out of trouble?" I asked, smiling embarrassedly, praying that my lack of restraint hadn't spoiled the rest of our vacation together.

"Your tongue is beautiful and your words are very welcome, sister. Never change," he replied.

I love him. Very much.

"Thank you. Thank you." I said.

"And yet?" I asked after a moment of silence and heartwarming smiles.

"So," asked Nadav, "are you saying that everyone is beautiful in your eyes?"

"No."

"I thought that…" he continued and I stopped him.

"You're innocent until proven otherwise, right? At least, as far as I'm concerned."

"Meaning? Please explain it to the ignorant person that I am."

"Please stop." I was sure he was being cynical.

"No, come on, translation, please; I think I understand what you mean; still, it's interesting hearing it from you."

"Someone's inner colors are the colors you eventually see outside. To me, personality changes appearance, even though it doesn't actually change at all. I don't think I invented the wheel." I got defensive, not wanting to sound stupid. But I was stupid to feel like I had to be defensive. I didn't like how my mind went straight to the negative.

"True. It isn't new, But this is the first time I've met someone for whom it's a reality and not just a cliché," Nadav said seriously.

"A person can be seen as beautiful or ugly, no matter what his external appearance – it all depends on who he is inside. So I think that, if we must be critical, then that's what we can criticize and, even then, with caution."

Nadav was silent, looking at the sand as he patted it with his foot.

"Apologies, I didn't mean to be boring or burdensome."

"Not a chance! Boring or burdensome?" he said in the voice of someone carrying a heavy load on his back. Slowly he bent down.

"Thank you. Even if you don't mean it."

"But I do," he replied in the same choked voice.

"Okay, okay, I understand. Stop being so cynical, you know what I meant."

"I think you're a beautiful soul," he said suddenly in a clear, decisive voice and straightened up.

"Thank you! You too," I said lovingly.

"You don't have to say it back."

"I'm not saying it back, I'm telling the truth." I continued in a more serious tone.

"You need to learn to accept compliments."

"I do have a hard time with that." I melted.

We stared towards the horizon for a moment; the sky was still pink and blue with remnants of the sun starting to shine on another place on the globe. Now it seemed as if someone had taken two brushes, one dipped in dark pink and one in blue, and brushed them both at the same time across the sky, creating a beautiful picture that was hard to look away from. We breathed it in deeply.

Suddenly I asked, "Do you think it's possible to turn fantasy into reality if we want to?"

"It depends," he said, "I haven't delved into it."

"I think we can create the fantasy we want, but it depends on us," I replied, completely sure of myself.

"When you put it that way, then I agree with you. Everything that depends on us and what we want is not a fairy tale. Will can definitely turn a fairytale into reality," answered Nadav, confident as well.

"Let's raise a toast: To turning the fairytale into reality." We raised our hands and clinked our imaginary glasses.

We laughed.

I felt like I wasn't alone anymore.

Mr. B. made me feel so alone in my ideas and thoughts when I shared them with him, until I just stopped telling him. He made sure to crush any positive thoughts I had.

When I said something similar to Mr. B., he said, "This isn't Hollywood, dreams don't come true,"

"Why shouldn't we create a better life for ourselves and for our wonderful children? I don't understand. It's our choice: to be happy with what we have or not to be, to do everything for each other or not to, to build our world better or not. What does it have to do with 'this isn't Hollywood?'

"Do we need to be in Hollywood in order for us to realize the dreams that depend on us? Besides, what I said should be a way of life, not a fantasy. Is it a fantasy to decide to live well together?"

How did I miss that the situation wasn't good, not good at all?

We reached the deck. For a moment, I looked towards the horizon to my right and saw Ben. He stood his hands in his pockets. His stance was firm. His gaze was on me.

"Are you coming, dear?" asked Nadav, sure of my answer.

"In a moment," I replied.

"Is everything okay?" he asked, checking to see what had occupied my gaze.

"So, Franklin draws attention, right? I admit: I was wrong about him. You were right. He's a perfectly decent guy," he said, smiling. He smiled and meant it.

I hope so, I thought to myself, I don't have the energy to be disappointed again. From people I mean.

"Wait," Nadav said as I started to move towards Ben. "I'll take Anch."

"Thank you," I looked at the big clock in the living room.

"If I get delayed, could you please check if the pie and kugel are ready? They're supposed to be ready in about ten minutes." I have no idea where that question came from. It isn't like me to ask for things. I do everything on my own.

"Yes. Of course." Nadav replied so naturally that I didn't feel uncomfortable at all.

"You stick a toothpick…" I start explaining.

"Are you serious?" said Nadav, smiling, and gave me a wink.

I climbed the stairs to the deck of Ben's balcony. He was looking at me and then the horizon.

"And what are you carrying around?" I asked, tenderly and very carefully, yet assertively to get an answer.

"Gail was six at the time and David was three. He was in a constant race to catch up with the three-year gap that Gail had experienced without him. Gail was very much looking forward to the trip. We had been to see the Statue of Liberty when she was younger. Still, she was excited to go back there as if it was her first time. 'This time, I'll remember it,' she said. That day I had to leave very early for a meeting. Daina, Gail and David were supposed to arrive later and we were supposed to meet. Daina suggested that we surprise her brother Michael, who had an office on the 100th floor of the South Tower. We'd never met. What happened in the buildings could be seen from the road where she was driving and, in a moment of distraction, that terrible accident happened. In one single moment, nine years ago, my life collapsed.

Ben stopped talking, his eyes shining. Did I understand what happened? Or maybe not? Could it be?

I wanted to hug him to me. I don't know why I didn't do it. Maybe because Mr. B. came out a liar, and society would see him as a good man and a wonderful husband, and he was neither of those. I don't know what kind of life he and Daina had before that terrible accident. Oh. How terrible. How terrible.

Why do I think so? Ben is wonderful. Not everyone is Mr. B. I don't know. I don't know whether to trust my intuitions now.

I'm not as naïve as I used to be. I learned the hard way to pay attention to things.

"Why the guitar?" I asked, my eyes filling up with tears.

Why did I even ask about the guitar? I couldn't find anything to say other than asking about the guitar?!

"Gail loved the guitar. 'Daddy, I want to play like you. Teach me,' she would plead, full of life and wonder. 'When your hands grow. I promise. In the meantime, we'll play together,' I replied, and we'd sit together, having fun trying."

"I don't need anything," he said, pausing. Then he continued, "I want them back! All the time! My life. I should have been with them! We should have gone together."

How sad! That's why he's alone all the time! Doesn't want the company of others! Surely afraid to hurt them; surely interprets being happy with others as being disloyal to them. He wants only their company, even if it is only in his memories. They're enough for him.

"Everyone has their own path in this life," I couldn't explain, it was beyond my ability, but I wanted to say something, to strengthen him, because there is nothing that could be said to be a comfort in such a situation.

"I couldn't go on living in our house anymore. I turned it into a memorial. I also commemorated it online so everyone would know what a wonderful family they were. Beloved.

"Everything stands the same as the day they left the house. On the tables, I placed all the birthday cards, holiday cards, and love letters I had written to my wife over the years, which she kept in the drawer in the white commode in the hallway under the second-floor stairs. I wanted her to feel courted and loved all the time, especially after the wedding. I made sure to surprise her with love letters written on letterhead, as they used to do in old times. I was excited to see her flushed face every time she read a letter I left in the mailbox. I'd wait in the car to see her smile when she found the envelope."

Ben threw his head between his palms, pulling his hair tightly back between his fingers as he leaned with his elbows against the railing of the balcony.

"I wanted them to have nothing but good in their lives, everything I could do, for Daina, for Gail, for David," Ben paused. He couldn't talk anymore.

"I'm sure Daina had a wonderful life with you, the best there is, she felt loved and appreciated. Gail and David also felt loved and knew how dear they were to you; they understood that you gave them a whole world of nothing but good. They had a good life, even if it was short. I am very sorry. I'm so sorry," I said, my voice choking. I wanted to cry, but I stopped myself.

I believe that the soul remains, but this was not the time to say it. Life never ends. When a door closes, a different one opens. Sometimes we meet again at the new entrance, sometimes we don't. My opinion has been settled on this matter and I believe I understand how things work. Although I have no way of verifying it, one thing is clear beyond any doubt: that true and deep love will lead souls to meet again.

So much pain. How can it be overcome? It is very difficult to find light in such darkness. Longing will know no end and there is no way of bringing them back. Oh! Oh! What bad people there are in the world! The story of Noah teaches that the correction of the world will come from the people, "for a man's desire is evil from his youth," so that if everyone corrects the wrong within him, the world will no longer be broken, it will be good. In my innocence, for years, I believed that if everyone understood that, everyone would embrace it and the world would be corrected. I didn't understand, nor could I imagine that there are bad people who don't want others to have good. Otherwise, they would be preoccupied with their lives, creating and thinking about how to improve themselves and wouldn't create problems for others.

Though, on the other hand, I understood the force that gave him the will to get up in the morning. His love for them. For him, it happened yesterday; they live inside him right now. Every word I say will seem superfluous.

Now that I could verify what he had said, I really wanted to hug him. He deserved then and deserves now to be loved. I appreciated his loyalty to his family, for his ability to love like that, and his devotion. I took his hand and held it tightly. Then I brought him closer to me and hugged him. He hugged me back, gently supporting my back. I hugged him tightly and wrapped him with all my soul, as much as I could, to transfer my energy to him, to protect him.

"You're such a good soul, dear Ben, you are a good and special soul. I wish there were many more people like you, who knew how to love like this, to give their loved ones everything they need," I said. I hurt a lot for him, for his family. "Your family was blessed to have you; you made them happy. And besides, we never really die. They will always love you." Ben tightened his grip on me and pulled me closer to him.

It's hard not to trust people. I have to trust my intuition and the lessons life has taught me over the past two years. Not everyone is Mr. B. My intuitions were right about Ben, Nadav and Ari as well. I am ok. I am ok. I'll trust myself.

CHAPTER 9

08.23.2010

*L*ast night, before I went to sleep, I got into bed and looked to the sky, to the horizon, like every night since we got here. I thought about everything Ben had said and remembered that Mr. B. once took my hands and said to me, "Are these a woman's hands? These are the hands of a child. Go get a manicure." I wanted to answer him: 'These are the hands of your wife who makes you soup when you're sick, bake cakes for you when you ask for them, and even when you don't, make sure your clothes are always clean, and cover you at night when the blanket falls off. These are the hands on which you put a ring and, with it, you sanctified me to you as your wife. Can't you see all this in them?! Has your vision become so limited? Is there nothing left of your soul because of this betrayal? I wanted to remind you how much these hands are still doing by raising our two precious children with endless, unconditional love and without a desire for anything in return, but it certainly didn't interest him because he is the center of his world, his life revolves around himself. "I am my own center, I only care for myself." I thought I misheard him. What do the children have to do with all this? As far as he's concerned... any explanation I had to help the situation, to try to correct it, to enlighten him about the terrible mistake he was making, that afterward, it would be very difficult to correct, if at all, but he didn't want to hear. The new conditions under which I would live from now on. I am not allowed to express my opinion or explain my wishes, as it will become a speech and he is no longer willing to hear speeches; and the truth is that, at some point, I also did not want to try harder for him. I wanted it all to end. Mainly, I wanted him to leave us. The terrible soul that he had adopted for himself could not become part of my life, I could not contain it in any way, I could not love a person who sees himself as the center of his life. How could the children be treated like this? They don't deserve it! They didn't do anything to deserve it. I don't deserve it either! I hate him for that, so very much.

It took me a long time to realize that he wasn't Michael Douglas and we weren't in Fatal Attraction. I thought I would help him. I was empathic to the character played by Douglas, not justifying his infidelity, but he really loved his wife, didn't want her to get hurt, didn't want her to know about the mistake he made, he wanted to keep her from all that sorrow. Mr. B. didn't care at all about protecting me or the children. On the contrary, he just brought it home, more and more, and desecrated the temple I built for us. No respect. No compassion. No responsibility. I would've appreciated him if he had packed his clothes and belongings and left, apologizing for what happened and accepting and understanding whatever I decided. Moreover, he never took care of the children, he wasn't there most of the time, and why should we pay for his mistakes? They shouldn't shape our lives.

How lucky Daina is… was… how attractive Ben seemed after he told her all he felt for her and what he did for them. A very beautiful relationship, his intentions were pure, even if there was a problem, it would have been forgiven immediately because, in his heart, there was only good and only love. Such nobility, how can it not captivate a woman's heart? Their love was sacred, the connection spiritual; even when he goes on, alone, she will be with him, protect him from wherever she is. From all bad. Give him the whole world and put it in the palm of his hand. Words have such power and love is so powerful that there isn't an obstacle that cannot be overcome. I'm sure Daina was willing to die for him.

Well, not that that's what happened. Enough.

What did I want? Not to be ignored. To love my husband and protect him from all evil and for him to love me and protect me from all evil. To build together a warm and loving home for us and for the children we'll have and raise. What did I ask for? What did I ask for? It's not in the stars, it's in our hands. Within our reach. However, I was the only one participating in this relationship.

What happened to this husband who married me? Where did he go? As if they had replaced him with another. Too bad. Too bad he doesn't appreciate things that aren't bought with money. My mother used to say that a person earns money and that money comes and goes, but there are things that go and never come back and they have to be cherished. It's good to have money, but it's a means, not an end. When the heart is in the right place, the goal is achieved and the means are piled up abundantly. Mr. B. had a notepad, which also took me time to understand. His giving, if it could even be called that, was marked down and recorded, like an accounting chart.

The phrase 'one man can set fire to an entire forest' is truer than the opinion that 'it takes two to tango.' I know from experience that one can do the job entirely on his own. One is enough to destroy.

From now on, I won't leave Ben. I am like he is with me, want to compensate him. It's clear to me that it's not possible, but whatever I can do to make him even a little bit happy will be worth the effort. I will not give up on him and I will make sure that he is present at every event and outing that we all have together. I think I'll update Nadav and Ari as well and they will surely understand and comply, with sensitivity.

I need to think about it.

CHAPTER 10

08.28.2010

Unfortunately, I learned that life is unpredictable and there is no black and white. In many cases, there's another color, a mixture of the two: gray, a confusing and exhausting color.

You could have a calm and peaceful life and then, suddenly, without any warning, your world can turn upside down. Some people immediately grasp what kind of storm they've been caught up in, while others, like me, don't yet understand that they are in a storm. Moreover, when they do understand, they don't realize how strong it is, how it changes all existing order, as storms do. They don't yet understand its implications. We went today to visit our home in the city and to take some things we forgot. We noticed we forgot them only when we needed them; it's a good thing we needed them before the flight.

We were happy to return, but also saddened. We missed home. The children ran into their room to look for the things they had forgotten. It amazed them how small the house had become. Me too. We remembered it bigger.

I stood in our bedroom. From the window, even though they were far away, three skyscrapers were visible. I missed my husband. I missed the husband who married me, the one who had a healthy sense of humor, who spoke kindly in a pleasant and sensitive tone, the one who was dear to my heart. It seems like he always had one thing on his mind and another in his heart, but I didn't understand that. I thought what he showed and did was what he truly felt. I didn't understand why he told me, one of the times he yelled at me, "I'm done with this. I'm not walking on eggshells anymore." I didn't understand what eggshells he had to walk on. I thought he was like me. That when I love, I love, and when I don't, I don't. When I'm happy, I'm happy, and when I'm sad, I'm sad. My feelings and my appearance are one and the same, my external expression matches my internal emotions. Angry, disappointed, mostly at myself, that I was stupid.

The first evening we spent together, the first time we met, was in November: a pleasant and breezy night. I remember exactly what we were wearing. I wanted to go to the Old City, to the port nearby. It was a blind date and I was afraid I wouldn't have anything to talk to him about, so I preferred to walk rather than sit in a café face to face. We walked. We were almost on our own. The wind blew, causing the masts to tap each other. Mr. B. told me about Andromeda and then about Napoleon. I knew about Andromeda, but I didn't know about Napoleon and his soldiers. He was well-versed in stories from the past. It was a wonderful evening. We enjoyed being together. Mr. B. was interesting, nice, and very polite. He was very determined to be in a relationship with me and stuck with me from that evening on, not even letting me go to the university library without him. I was very independent and uncomfortable with this clinginess, but I appreciated his determination and thought it was just important to him to be with me every moment. Once again, my instincts were wrong. I interpreted everything in a positive light and thought he had a clear plan.

I wasn't completely blind, I also saw some sides that I didn't like. But I thought that if Mr. B. loved me so much then surely those sides would disappear. However, not only they did not disappear, but they got worse.

When I think about it now, I didn't want to lose Mr. B., the idea of him, the person I thought he was. Yet there were days when I thought the only right step was divorce. I couldn't stand the complaints and accusations anymore and still feel the sting of the knife thrust in my back. He made no effort to increase the light at all, to remove the darkness; on the contrary, he made sure to exacerbate it. I was scared. If we didn't have children, I wouldn't be afraid at all, I wouldn't think twice, I wouldn't have given him a second chance, certainly not to someone who has no regrets. My heart broke when I thought about divorce. I had to remember that I'm not giving up on the person I married, but rather, I had to remember that he was never who I thought he was. No. That's not true. I'm angry. Enough. My children are the product of love and they make everything ok. For now, things will stay this way. When they're old enough not to be obligated to custody arrangements, I'll sort my life out.

Successes make me happy and fill my heart, even if they're not mine. It has always made me happy to see others succeed. First of all, for them and then for me, because it proved that such a thing is possible. On top of that, I was at peace with myself and I had the confidence that, one day, I too would have the success I longed for. Success makes me happy, yes, even when it belongs to others. Why shouldn't it? May all who want good things have only good things.

I stepped out of our bedroom, stopped and looked at the bathroom, which seemed large mainly because of the view from its window as well as from the other windows; I ended up in the children's bedroom. How many nights I didn't sleep because of my dear ones' illnesses and how worried I was for them to recover and be okay. Come to think of it, I was so busy taking care of and raising our children that I didn't notice the nasty way Mr. B. had been treating me most of the time.

Einstein said: "Only a life lived for others is a life worthwhile." Living for your family is no shame. After all, your family is you and you are your family, no matter how you look at it. A family doesn't cancel you, it empowers you, even more so the one you choose to establish yourself.

Why am I explaining to myself what is already clear to me? Any sensible person understands it. The problem is his, not mine. Only he doesn't understand it. Maybe he's really under the influence of some drug. He's really not the same person he used to be.

I need to stop being confused! By him. By everything that happened. By everything that's happening.

I have to make a choice and go with it, wholeheartedly. To act wisely now and later. I have to.

"Shall we go, children?" I asked. I tried to sound happy, hiding all the feelings, thoughts and pain.

At the exit from the building, we met the neighbors who were as pleased to see us as we were to see them.

On the way home, with the soundtrack of Shrek playing in the background, I thought: People don't understand me most of the time. Ari, Nadav and Ben are truly exceptions. I often find myself squirming, downplaying my values so as not to hurt or embarrass anyone, so they won't feel threatened by me. But that's not how things happen when I take a stand for things that are important to me, or especially to my children, then I'm very clear and sometimes sound very rude, even though that's not my intention at all. Why am I bringing this up now? Because as I passed by my children's school, I remembered how Nelly's third-grade teacher kept misinterpreting what I said and how much grief she caused us. Maybe now that I've become sober about other matters, it's not that she didn't understand me, she didn't *want* to understand me. Questions or innocent statements such as, 'Aren't you making the mat exercise too difficult for them?' or 'Should I check with the Ministry of Education what the subjects for these classes are?', the teacher saw as a threat. I'm sure that she wouldn't have signed a loan at the bank, no matter how nice the teller was, without checking that the terms promised to her are on the form she is asked to sign.

I need to check, to avoid mistakes, I don't want to regret it later. Regardless, I don't have to explain the desire for things to be correct. What's wrong with wanting them to be done right?

People say you have to let children deal with things on their own and not defend them all the time. It's true, but the question is when and how? To bring a child into the world and throw him into the deep end? He may learn to swim out of fear, but he may also drown. In addition, what kind of experience is it to learn things out of fear? I brought children into the world because I wanted them and I wanted to raise them and love them, guide them, be there for them and especially to make sure they had as good a life as I could give them. At least as much as I'm able. Why throw them into the deep end on their own? We will enter together and carefully, we will learn the right movements so that we may be able to float and not drown, we will practice and then they'll can continue on their own. A parent is always a parent: even when the child is swimming alone, the parent is watching from a distance.

CHAPTER 11

08.30.2010

While walking with Anch today, I remembered a very good friend I once had who told me, in these very words, "You have to screw the boys; that's the only way they appreciate you." We were 18 years old at the time. I disagreed with her. Today, when I think about it, maybe without realizing it, a son is looking for a woman who will be the essence of his mother. So if his mother was tough with him, he'll probably look for a woman who'll be tough with him, and if he had good communication with his mother, he will look for someone with whom it is easy to communicate. I don't see Neil looking for a woman who'll screw him over in order to appreciate her, he'll appreciate her if she's sensitive to him, listens to him without playing games, honest, loving and genuine – no power plays, no trickery. Maybe someone whose mother forced him to do things she thought he should; maybe he really should have, maybe he shouldn't, only he knows what is right for him. Let's get back to the point: she didn't give in even when he cried and, when he finally did what she demanded of him, he received a hug and love from her. That's a man who'll get along with a woman who'll 'screw him over.' He'll also do what he doesn't want just so that, in the end, he'll be treated lovingly by her. Well, I'm not like that. What was good for Mr. B. was good for me. Why waste your life arguing? Instead, you can enjoy every moment, plan trips abroad, embark on personal challenges, experience things together and separately, constantly get wiser, develop yourself, discover new things, together or separately, from a very clear, obvious starting point, and not hurt each other.

It's good that I still have an opinion that's stayed rather consistent. I mustn't get lost again, I must not get confused anymore. Most scary of all is losing your way.

In any case, if she was right and, in order to have a man who will love and appreciate me, I need to 'screw him over', then I'll probably stay alone. It doesn't come naturally to me to screw someone over and I also don't want to change for someone to stand by me, who also ends up being screwed up. What kind of relationship would that be? I want a loving man by my side, not a screwed-up one. Why must he be screwed up like that to love me? What? Is he stupid? He just needs to love. Just love! To understand me and not what he wants to understand. To be a friend who really listens and gets me. To feel like we're equals, not to feel like he must prove, in the eyes of his wife and his friends, who wears the pants at home. In any case, what is this nonsense about who wears the pants at home? Scots sometimes where kilts, can have a loving wife, and still seem to be good, strong, sensitive men.

Before the problems started, we received two tickets to a play as a gift from Mr. B.'s parents who had a theatre subscription. We went to 'Defending the Caveman', a comedy that turned out to be an excellent show. It was so fascinating and amusing that the two hours seemed more like a few minutes and, apart from the subject of the closet, which wasn't true for us because Mr. B. had much more clothes than I did, everything that was said appeared very on point for both of us. On second thought, now that everything has come to light, perhaps not completely.

Taking the premise that men have been hunters since the dawn of history and, therefore, concentrate on only one thing, in the case of Mr. B., it applies only when it suits him; apparently, he can be the gatherer as well when he wants to, a supposedly female characteristic. If he had been a hunter by nature, I'm sure we wouldn't be in this place today. I'm tired. To me, everything is much simpler: black is black and white is white, why do they need to be mixed?? I think that people who understand gray can't see that white is only white and black is only black. It didn't confuse me. I don't think it has to be so complex.

There is no doubt that I have changed. The way I keep rummaging through what happened. As the Yiddish saying goes: "Don't put a healthy head in a sick bed." This used to be clear to me and I used to be able to set boundaries.

On the other hand, it's good that I repeat it over and over again so that maybe I won't make the same mistake again, I'll be sure of what I want and need. And what do I want and need? Someone who'll be sensitive to my needs as well, not just his own, especially without me having to say explicitly what they are. Someone who has the ability to separate the essential from the marginal, someone who will love me for my way of thinking, for my choices, for my intentions, for my friendship with him.

Mr. B. twisted everything around. Ben is probably right, everything is getting sorted out now. Mr. B. had bad character traits and he didn't want to be the only one drowning, so he pulled me down with him.

I want to believe that there is more to him, that there is some inner conflict in him, a war between good and evil, between stupidity and selfishness and wisdom and giving. But it's hard for me to credit him at the moment, his stupidity and selfishness won too many times.

Maybe I'm the problem. My patience, tolerance, and my belief that, in the end, good will prevail over evil may not be virtues after all.

Maybe whoever is good is good and whoever is bad is bad, and whoever contains both and chooses evil most of the time is lost and there is no hope for him.

No! I won't believe it! I believe it's all a choice, I want to choose to be courteous and pleasant, so I'll be courteous and pleasant, just as I choose which bread to buy at the bakery. The former seems easier to me than the latter, because a person doesn't require external means, only their own sense of right and wrong.

Interestingly, the support I gave him whenever he was insecure, such as: "I'm with you no matter what," "I don't care how much you earn as long as you're happy," "We live once, as far as we know, so I want you to live well and not end up regretting it," "You can do anything you want, you are very capable and you have special qualities that others don't have." I meant every word I said. And all that wasn't enough to prove my friendship and loyalty. However, if I had manicures and pedicures, a new hairstyle and wasted the money we didn't have at the time, then he would have valued my friendship more.

Stupid and shallow imbecile.

"Do you want coffee?" I heard Nadav's pleasant voice.

"No thanks," I replied. His question brought light to my dark thoughts.

"Are you sure? I make delicious coffee," Nadav said, his face lighting up.

"I'm sure. Just being in your company is enough. I'll make tea," I said.

"No, I will," Nadav said.

"No, it's okay; I know how I like it. Thank you," I said.

"Then tell me how you like it and I'll make it for you," Nadav insisted.

"It's really okay," I insisted.

"I insist," he said and took down the tea boxes from the cupboard. "So which one do you like?"

Maybe I died and went to heaven, perhaps at the beginning of the summer.

Maybe this is normal. Maybe it's normal and what we had wasn't normal. So abnormal that I think you have to die and go to heaven in order to live like this.

"This one," and I handed him a tall pinkish porcelain cup.

"How much water?" asked Nadav.

How did he even know to ask? I like my tea strong so I don't fill the glass.

"Three-quarters. Thank you."

"Don't mention it, darling." You're a darling yourself, I should have told him.

"Yes, I will." I persisted. For showing me that there's another way, that life can be easy, for seeing my children and me as we deserved, for making me feel important, insisting on making me a cup of tea. Thank you for being such a great person. I wanted to tell him all that but I didn't say a word.

As close as I feel to him and Ari, I prefer to keep it to myself; burdening others won't ease my burden. Even if it would, I wouldn't burden them with my problems.

While Nadav was preparing our drinks, I asked him, "Do you think there is such a thing as love that isn't dependent on anything?"

Nadav didn't answer at first. After a moment, he said in a quiet tone.

"Wow. That's a big question."

"Yes." I smiled. "And yet?"

"I need a moment to think about it."

I took out the cakes I made last night and sliced them. Poppy cake and cheesecake with brown sugar and cinnamon frosting.

"Your cakes are very tasty," Nadav said, taking a bite of the poppy cake. I really like the poppy cake as well.

"Thank you," I smiled again. Lucky for me I don't blush.

"I'm sure you can having people lining up, if you want."

"I thought about it once when we needed the money. I used to receive compliments on my cakes and I thought I'd give it a try."

"So why didn't you?"

"I was afraid that if people ordered from me, my cakes would burn or dry up or something else would go wrong."

I also didn't know how to price them. The truth is, I don't quite remember what tipped the scales not to move forward with the initiative. I tried to remember.

"No. I don't remember the reason. Can't remember why it didn't come to fruition. Neil must have had a fever, which jumped in an instant to 104 degrees. Advil didn't help, only compresses or a cool shower. Such a prince. He cooperated as if he understood that there was no choice. I explained it to him, but he could have also chosen not to understand and cooperate as he did. Such a darling child. He sat patiently, shivering in the cold bath or with the compresses in bed and let me take care of him." My heart clenched at the memory.

"It's true. Neil really is very special. A darling. It's easy to love them. Both of them. They have good souls."

"Thank you, beloved Nadav. You're a good soul too."

"Two perfect children," Nadav continued, "just like their mother."

"Thank you! But who they are is up to them. You'll see when you're a parent. You can lead, you can set an example but, in the end, they decide who they are." How did he know to compliment both of them? Not just one? And with exactly the same measure. I love him very much.

Nadav smiled, picked up the hot drinks and said, "Let's go outside and enjoy our drinks in the pleasant morning air and the cool sea breeze."

I took the sliced cakes and went out. I wanted to stop being immersed in energy-guzzling thoughts.

"I'll be back in a second," I said, hurrying into the kitchen. I remembered the rose tea from England that I received as a gift and hadn't used yet. I poured the rose mixture. Wow! The aroma of actual roses and I could already taste it before even taking a sip. I poured it into a charming jug with matching cups that I had saved for a special occasion. I'd used the set once before, when Nelly and I had tea at 4 p.m. – à la Alice in Wonderland. I organized everything on a tray and went back to the deck.

"What? Wow, what a delicious aroma. When did you have the time? You were gone for maybe half a second," Nadav wondered.

"Magic," I said, laughing. He's constantly making me feel wonderful, as if I'm doing extraordinary things. Thank the universe for both him and Ari.

We sat on the deck and the breeze was indeed pleasant and cool, gently playing with our hair and making our eyes tear.

After a sip of my tea, Nadav asked, "Well? Did it come out the way you like it?"

"Yes. Exactly. Thank you. You haven't answered yet: do you think there is love that doesn't depend on anything?"

"I was thinking about your question while the water was boiling. I've come to the conclusion that the only unconditional love is the one you have for your children. What do you think?"

"I think it depends on the person and not on a thing."

"What depends on the person and not on a thing?"

Ari suddenly arrived.

"Do you think there is a love that doesn't depend on anything?" Nadav asked Ari.

"I can't believe how deep you're going so early in the morning." Ari smiled at him.

"My fault. So, what's your answer?" I sincerely wanted an answer.

"That makes more sense," Ari said as he rubbed his eyes, brushed away some sleep. He sat down, smiled again and looked at Nadav. Nadav smiled too. "And I'd say you dropped a pretty heavy subject on us, sister," we all chuckled.

"Wow," Ari moved his face closer to the teapot, "so that's where the great smell of roses is coming from. You can taste it without actually drinking it." Ari said.

"Totally," I smiled.

"And? What do you think? Is there or isn't there?" I was interested in hearing his answer too.

"In my opinion, there is a true love that remains independent of anything." Ari replied, looking completely settled.

"Really? You surprise me!" said Nadav, sounding impressed.

"Why? What did you answer? That there isn't?" asked Ari, also surprised.

"What made you fall in love with Jenn?" Nadav asked Ari.

"I just loved her, I don't think it was anything in particular," Ari replied.

"I remember you saying: 'She was delicate and had an innocent look about her, like we had as little kids when we didn't know anything except to believe that we would one day reach the moon.' I'm almost certain these were your exact wording. It's impossible not to remember." Nadav said.

"I admit she had a sweet look, so innocent." Ari replied amused.

"So the question that arises now is: Where is she? Why isn't she here anymore?" asked Nadav, trying to prove a point.

"What's the connection, Nadav? After two months of being together, she decided she wanted to move to Iceland. You know..."

"And the innocent look became very angry and scary when you told her you couldn't join her." Nadav continued.

"And…?" Ari asked.

"So maybe the love for her stemmed only from the little girl's wishful look, and when it was gone…" Nadav was trying to prove that there's no love that doesn't depend on anything.

"Maybe this isn't a good example," Ari said thoughtfully, as if Nadav had a point.

"The question is whether there always is a motive and, if there is a motive, even if it isn't material, is it not a love that depends on something?" said Nadav confident in himself, a little cynical.

"Sorry for the question but, from what you just said, can I deduce that you aren't a couple?" I asked slowly and cautiously.

"Me and Mr. Socks-that-don't-go-in-the-washing-machine-for-a-week?" Ari asked.

"Don't exaggerate." Nadav defended himself.

"Not exaggerating at all." Ari insisted.

"We're misleading, aren't we?" asked Nadav.

"Yes. Very much. So you're not a couple?" I asked embarrassed.

"We're a couple, but not in that manner. I really love this lost Australian, but I'm not in love with him." Nadav replied.

Nadav and Ari laughed. What a direct question! Maybe I embarrassed them. "I love women, sorry. If not, I would have married you a long time ago, bro." Ari said.

"Really? We're both single now. You want to give it a try?" Nadav said, smiling, his eyes fixed on Ari.

Ari took a piece of poppy cake. "Why did you say it depends on the person and not a thing?"

"Because I think there are those who will love for no reason and there are those who will not love without reason."

"I think it's an emotion that has no explanation. It's just a feeling. You feel that you love or don't love and whoever looks for explanations won't find them because… it's an emotion… that you feel," said Ben. We all stared; it never happened that Ben joined the conversation of his own volition.

"That's because you're a person who just loves," I said.

"I agree with Ben," Ari said, "you saved us, brother; you formulated an excellent answer for us. Exhaustive," he told Ben. "Well done!" not cynically, he meant it.

"I don't think it depends on the person: there is always a reason and the 'reason' makes it depend on the thing," Nadav said, speaking while thinking, "Not everyone who falls in love knows how to separate it, to say, 'I love because' and when the 'because' disappears, to want to dismantle the package," Nadav said.

"Listen, brother, you're getting deep…" said Ari. "You're surprising today."

"Yes, surprising myself as well. What about a little praise? What's with you and this cynicism? What's got into you, Ari? Am I rubbing off on you? Wait, wait, here it is, the dismantling of the package," Nadav replied.

"I thought you said I was a heck of a friend," said an amused Ari.

"Maybe because Nadav's motive was your gentle manners?" I said. Of course, I was amused too, although the subject was very serious and important to me. I wanted to come out witty and cool and came out nerdy. I'm not at my best so I should think a little more before I speak!

"You know me, it's all in good faith. You're great, and it's good to have people like you in the world," Nadav said.

"Oh, so that's where the wonderful smell of roses is coming from," Ben said, bowing his head over the teapot. Tasty just from the smell." Ben smiled.

We all smiled. Such a wonderful person. We all wanted him to be happy.

"What do you think?" asked Ben, "does it depend on something or not?"

"I always thought that love should not depend on anything, love should be unconditional, which is a stronger emotion than any other emotion but, now, after our enlightening conversation, I think it is both: it depends on the person who loves and the personality of the one who is loved."

"For example…" said Nadav, waiting for me to elaborate.

"I'll explain it to you, dear bro," Ari hastened to reply. "Love depends on the personality of the beloved, but it also doesn't depend on anything, since the personality doesn't change."

"Doesn't it? I can say from experience that there are changes and even radical ones." Nadav said.

"So, from the beginning, you didn't read the map correctly or the map showed only the parts she wanted you to see and you, naively, believed that this was the whole picture." It was hard for me to say that; the explanation must have come from my bitter experience.

"She's right," Nadav said, "I told you that she had sides that you're better off not knowing about and that you should get away from her as soon as possible, but you were so sure of yourself, you said: 'You're not reading the situation well,' and, in the end, who didn't read it well?"

"Are we back to Jennifer again?" said Ari.

"Excuse me, aren't you a couple?" asked Ben in wonder.

"They are a couple but not like that," I answered for them.

"You too? Seriously?" said Nadav humorously, taking a piece of cheesecake.

"On the one hand, love is an unexplained emotion, mysterious and wonderful. On the other hand, love is not just an abstract idea. In the test of time, it is a result. Love does depend on something and, yes, it has conditions. It's clear. What was I thinking before? Of course, it's clear! Who would love someone who insults them? Doesn't appreciate them? Doesn't see them at all. Definitely, we fall in love with behavior; the wrapping is a bonus, no more than that. Of course, there has to be chemistry, a natural attraction, but again, the chemistry and attraction to someone is related to behavior." I said vigorously, sure of myself. It's scary how I suddenly grew up.

From the expressions and head movements, it seemed to me that everyone agreed with me. Now we all stared into the distance, at the meeting point between the blue of the sky and the blue of the sea. The sky was dark and, had I not known it was August, I would have thought it was going to rain. It was as if the sky had become serious, because such a question is not to be taken lightly and it is important that its answer be accurate and correct.

"Do you know your cakes are very delicious? You could sell them. no problem," Ari said.

"True, he's right," Ben added.

"Thank you," I said. I loved that Ben joined us without inhibitions and was part of us.

Again, we stared at the sea and enjoyed the idyllic tranquility and, although each was enjoying it alone, we felt that we were all together, no words needed. We enjoyed those moments of peace and grace, of beautiful colors, of primordial moments of harmony and perfection.

"Mom?"

"Yes?" I turned, "Come here, honey."

I look at Neil when he came towards me. I don't understand how Mr. B. could say that the children aren't the center of his life, and that he is the center of his life. The children are a major part of his life, but not the center and his life, which would never revolve around them.

I thought that, as parents who chose this role, we're always responsible for them, and since they are still young and still so dependent on us, it's very important that we stay by them, together. I understand now that it's as obvious to everyone as it is to me, but not to Mr. B. They'll grow up and they won't need us so much; they'll probably spend more time with their friends and then it will be okay for us to do more things without them, but Mr. B. wanted that now and didn't care if it was right or if I felt good about it or not, the only thing that mattered to him was him.

I don't do mani-pedis, I don't leave the kids with a babysitter so we can walk around in the middle of the day like a childless couple without commitment or responsibility. I wear black and I don't go to the hairdresser to style my hair and change its color. And apparently, my wishes don't matter; the main thing is that he wanted me to. I couldn't understand where we would get the money for all these luxuries. And what's wrong with giving up some things because our budget doesn't allow it? Because I did give those things up. But even if I didn't forego those things, I would have done them when the kids were hanging out with friends or busy with other activities, and certainly not in the way and frequency he expected. What's the fun of buying clothes, fixing my hair at the hair salon and getting a manicure if we end up with a negative balance at the end of the month? And then a few months later we'll have to take out another loan that we couldn't afford to pay back? How could I take pleasure in that? In the end, it was my fault that he went out and found someone to cheat with because, apparently, I wasn't his friend nor was I a good wife.

I just raised the children, alone. I don't complain because, to me, it's a privilege to raise my children. But alone? When there is a partner who can cuddle with you and watch as they grow up, admiring every smile or new word they say, an insight they come up with on their own.

I would encourage him when he was sad or disappointed about something, and I was happy with him and for him when he succeeded, trying to make him feel good about everything he wanted that would do him good; we were right there with him. When he went straight after work to colleagues' weddings or baby parties – there was no shortage of events that he attended – I didn't chastise him or complain that I was alone all day long, that the expenses were already high that month. He wouldn't even come home before going out; he would just take a change of clothes with him in the morning and stay at work until the event. I would have run home first, and I certainly wouldn't go to most of these things. I would just politely make an excuse.

I asked him every day when he was coming home so he would know that he's cared about and missed, and also so that I'd know when to prepare dinner for him. I was at home anyway so why not prepare his dinner too? We are family, aren't we? He's my husband, I want the best for him. But as it turns out, I'm not a friend, I'm a 'controlling woman.' A 'great wife' would be one who is manicured and pedicured, with colorful clothes and trendy hairstyles. Suddenly I'm also very short and my height hasn't changed since we met.

Also, how many events did he have in the summer before it all exploded? As if being home was such a burden to him, he had to find reasons to be out all the time and go to every event he was invited to.

Maybe he doesn't deserve another chance. Maybe he'll never be the person I wish for. If I were to write a book and tell readers these things, they would probably see me as an unreliable narrator; maybe even a science fiction writer, because how else could the mind and heart understand such ingratitude and egoism? How could a person behave like this?

When I think about it, all this nonsense he said after he went and found himself a girlfriend – maybe she was thin and tall with great nails and hair – I have no idea and I don't want to know what this adulterer looks like. I hoped that he would at least protect my honor and didn't gossip about me with her. This other woman also had children. What a fool! What a fool! Replacing his children with another's? She must have thought he was very rich. He always bought clothes and watches, in the latest styles, no less. According to what was dictated in men's magazines. Everything was so expensive, at least for us, with two average salaries and a mortgage, regular expenses for the house, the children. I used to add up all the expenses and let him know our budget, but he was never committed to sticking to what we could afford. He couldn't adhere to a framework. He couldn't delay gratification. First, we'll cut our expenses and, later on, we could take a breather. I don't know why he couldn't do as I explained. He knows how to delay gratification when he wants to. If he had a deadline for a work report, he wouldn't eat until he finished, even if it took him a few hours. He succeeded in losing a lot of weight two years ago. Now that I think about it, it seemed that whatever I said, he would do the opposite. Anyway, I didn't stop him from over-spending because I thought he needed it, even though it really annoyed me. Constantly afraid of what people would say about him in the company, plus he works for the money and you only live once. I should have told him. I should have told him that it annoyed me. I should have asked him: 'But didn't I tell you our budget? How can you buy all this?' The more I think about it, the more I realize how right Ben was; everything Mr. B. said was because he had to find bad things in me so he wouldn't feel bad about himself. Maybe now I can understand why every time we walked through the mall, although I would prefer to take a walk with the stroller near the house, he would urge me to buy clothes, even though I really didn't want to. I always had numbers running through my head, and buying new clothes wasn't an option with our budget. Even though I kept saying I didn't want to, he'd start nagging again and, eventually, I'd buy something because I thought, well, if it makes him happy. Obviously, I would love a new wardrobe, but not now when it's burdening us financially. When it is possible, and I can buy it wholeheartedly, I'll certainly be happy to do so. In any case, immediately after I bought something, he would also buy an outfit, he knew exactly which store to go into and what he was looking for. Now I understand he needed me to purchase something to justify his own expense. How did I come out the stupid one and not him? I hadn't thought about it before. I wasn't thinking at all. I had so many worries with the kids that I didn't have time to think. The truth is that, even if I had, I wouldn't have realized it was a ruse. I trusted him completely. Ben was right about everything. He was really looking to make me the one who was wrong to justify his betrayal: I'm a bad woman; I turn over the sunny-side-up egg to make sure there's no salmonella, even though he doesn't want it turned. I added brown sugar to his coffee instead of sweetener because brown sugar is better than artificial sweetener. Apparently, it makes me a controlling woman. How did he confuse caring with control?

So many energy-consuming thoughts and it wasn't even nine a.m. yet. Why do I need all this? I have to stop or I'll find myself in the express lane to the grave, and I can't stand the thought of leaving the children in his treacherous hands. I realize I have to stop. I have to. Maybe I don't understand it all, even though I think I've cleverly figured everything out and now I understand very well.

Ari, Nadav, Ben and Neil found something to talk about together; they decided to try the rose tea, which was delicious even without drinking it. How good it is for me now. I've felt this way all summer. The idyllic atmosphere has given me time to think.

"Good morning," I heard Nelly.

"Good morning, beautiful." Nadav said to Nelly. I love him so much!

Nelly sat and joined us at the table.

Neil immediately offered Nelly the rose tea. I'll try it too. Ari got ahead of me and poured for Nelly and me.

We were so happy with the attention and the kind words that we didn't notice we were drinking the tea without sugar. When the heart is full, the food definitely becomes secondary. When the heart is full of worries it can become comforted with food; or it can be full of love and have no room left for food. Ours right now was full of love. My Nell and Neil, like me, were very emotionally satisfied.

I baked vanilla cookies and chocolate cake to take with us to the amusement park in the afternoon.

I love baking; I love cooking as well. First, I make food how I like it. Secondly, I enjoy that others enjoy it and I'm also happy to receive compliments on how delicious it was. Third, it takes creativity and creating, in itself, is quite pleasurable.

I've noticed that when I'm scared, I lose my appetite and I begin to bake. Preparing delicacies, especially baking, gives me peace of mind. In addition to the compliments, I think I bake a lot because, the more I bake, the more the fear will disappear. It gives me a sense of control over my life: I can be creative and create delicious things and, if I can do that, maybe I can even change the situation that has been created in my life and make it better.

In the afternoon, we went to the amusement park and Ruth and the kids joined us as well. When I started the car, 'We are the World' was playing on the radio: 'We are the world, we are the children, we are the ones who make a brighter day, so let's start giving. There's a choice we're making, we're saving our own lives. It's true we'll make a better day just you and me.' Although the words of the song were written for a different purpose, they are suitable for the whole world at any time and they are so true, especially for my life now. I thanked the universe for strengthening me once again, this time through a song on the radio. From now on, I'll be completely available to pay attention to signs. I will never again bang my head against the wall, which is completely unnecessary because, not only was the wall not breached, but it only lead to headaches and confusion. I want to go on the roller coaster. For years I've been scared of riding roller coasters, a fear I didn't know before giving birth to Nelly.

Fear took over and took up a lot of space. Nelly was born with spherocytosis. The hematologist told me when she was four months old – she'd already been diagnosed by then – that this was the reason for the destruction of the red blood cells and the decrease in hemoglobin – and that it was important to pay attention that she avoid hemolysis. The meaning, in cases of infants born with spherocytosis, is a rapid breakdown of red blood cells, faster than the body can replace them. "Why?" I asked. "What could happen?" I remember the hematologist lingering with the answer.

"Can it cause death?" I kept asking, very frightened.

"Yes," he replied.

I intended to protect my children in every way, from the moment I saw them until forever but, with that diagnosis, I was ten times more alert and I never had a moment without worries. Nelly had a special blood type and, in general, she destroyed more red cells than she produced. A wonderful homeopath saved us; she was a magician; the treatment she gave Nelly in drops and pills was very demanding but also helped a lot because, since we started using it, she no longer needed blood transfusions. How bad I felt when Nelly had a fever or a virus, I kept checking the path between her scalp hairs and the conjunctiva of her eyes to see their color because I knew how to identify if the hemoglobin was too low and if a blood test was needed; and when the pallor appeared, the homeopathic treatment was even more demanding and, instead of giving it four times a day, I had to add another treatment every half hour. I administer the treatment as if it didn't require any effort from me, the goal justified the means, I could not bear another attempt to find a vein in her pale little arm, stab after stab and the crying. I was helpless; I couldn't explain to her why they were doing this to her, and I couldn't calm her down or help her. The first tap in her arm was at the age of two weeks, and thank goodness that from the age of four months, the nightmare stopped, thanks to the homeopathic medicines. In third grade, there was no choice; her spleen was extremely large, and there was a risk of it exploding, even from a slight fall on the stomach, so we went into surgery. Nelly was so brave and wonderful throughout it all, from the moment I explained the surgery to the removal of the stitches. The splenectomy, a two-and-a-half-hour operation, during which I couldn't breathe out of fear, went well. In the end, it was laparoscopic surgery; they succeeded without opening the abdomen. I breathed a sigh of relief. Recovery was easier, relatively speaking. To this day, I check Nelly's middle hairline, without her noticing, to see that it doesn't pale even though it's already very much behind us. Mr. B. noticed me checking it out and told me I had nothing to worry about, it wouldn't come back. He had it too, he knows.

I decided I had to get on the roller coaster. I have to face my fears!

On the way to the roller coaster, we bought delicious hot corn and sat down for a moment on a bench so I could find the cold drinks in my bag. On the bench next to us sat a couple with a small child, about four years old. The father got up several times to follow the boy to give him another bite of the sandwich that they apparently brought with them from home. The mother sat on the bench the whole time.

I sat on the roller coaster. I didn't ask Ruth if she wanted to join me because she didn't seem like the roller coaster type. And anyway, who'd stay with the kids on the ground? I also felt I had to do it on my own. However, as soon as I entered the roller coaster car, I got out. Then I went back and asked to go up again. I was debating with myself: what if I have a heart attack? No, I won't have one. Everything is fine, I'm strong, I'll handle it perfectly. Nothing will happen.

We had a great time at the amusement park. In the end, I didn't ride the roller coaster. Just the thought of having a heart attack and leaving the children with Mr. B. tipped the scales.

I'll find a safer way to overcome the fear, I don't want it to control me anymore.

At night, when I put the last things in my suitcase, I thought about the couple sitting on the bench next to us today. I've thought about relationships a lot and now I think, if I collect everything I've seen and heard and felt, with us and others over the years, that a relationship is like a ball full of rice flakes.

I imagined a transparent ball. That the line which connects its two semicircles, although transparent, could be seen. The ball is half-full of rice flakes. The rice flakes are the love, the giving and the responsibility. Each hemisphere is one partner. Now, when we roll the ball and it eventually comes to a stop, we can see that the rice flakes will be divided differently between the two sides of the ball.

In every couple, there is one who behaves more responsibly, gives more and loves more but, if the other took more upon himself, then the first would do less. The flakes are equally present in every relationship, but are often divided unevenly. It all depends on how much each partner is giving, loving and responsible. True success is a couple that finds balance in all those rice flakes and who knows how to complete and appreciate one another.

I believe that responsibility, giving and love are shared energies in any healthy relationship. One takes on more and the other naturally balances and takes on less. It could've just as well been the other way around. I don't know if balancing is the right word, it's more like allowing yourself because you know you can trust your partner.

In our case, I was the one who did the worrying for both of us.

I don't need thanks, of course not, but neither do I need contempt and ridicule.

I think I saw the relationship like a ballet dance.

In one of the lectures I attended, I learned that, in its early days, ballets didn't give an artistic role to the man. The woman was the artist, the dancer, while the man's role was to be there to support and assist her.

I found that the role of the man is actually significant and highly valued. The woman was the one who danced, true, but the man, although he did not play an artistic role on stage, was the one who was strong, one who stood by and guarded and was there when the woman needed support during the dance. On the surface, it seemed that the man's role in the dance was marginal but, in fact, the woman couldn't perform all of the moves without him.

I saw such a relationship as perfect: I will do what is necessary and more, because I love to give, it comes voluntarily, not out of necessity, and I don't keep score. Friendship can't be measured in a ledger. All I need from my partner is for him to be strong, to guard, protect and support, emotionally and physically, whatever the situation requires, without competition and power games or a notepad, because only this way I could see him as a real man, and only then could I love him with all my heart.

CHAPTER 12

08.31.2010

*I*t was a day very uncharacteristic for the end of August. Everything was covered by fog. The beach, the sea and, even the deck were covered in a white mist. If I didn't know better, I would have walked until I entered the water, and I would have been surprised to find that there was a sea here. The sea was there and so was the beach, but you couldn't see more than your own feet and the next step.

It's a pity, I thought to myself, I wanted to once again see the clear blue of the sea and the sky reflecting in them, the bright horizon, to feel the peace and beauty, the belonging, the harmony.

The fog was cool. White. Mysterious. On one hand, it arouses fear by obstructing vision but, on the other, an excitement with the magic that it brings. It was amusing to imagine that there was a gate to another place further along and not the sea, which was no longer visible.

This time the suitcases were not sent a day in advance. I had no problem taking them with me on the day of the flight, I preferred less logistics and more peace of mind.

We had a great summer. It was 62 days of insights.

I approached the deck as I wanted to reach the palm trees that gave this place a magical look and a feeling of an oasis, full of vegetation in all its shades, its colors combining in a wonderful harmony.

Walking through the fog, everything around me was white. How strange and exciting, as if I was really inside a cloud.

I reached the palm trees, and here they were, as if in a painting that begins with them and, from this point, we need to add more details on the white, clean canvas.

I thought of my dear parents. How good it is to remember them.

I remembered that in fifth grade, interestingly, when I was Nelly's age, my dear mother bought me a hardcover diary and told me, "Write down what you're going through every day, what happens to you and, one day when you grow up you'll be able to read it and remember what used to be." How did I forget about that?!

As the youngest child, maybe it was important to my mother that I write everything down because when she said, "I don't know if I'll still be around tomorrow," she also meant it and so, just in case one day she won't be here to remind me who I am, the diary will.

Dear Mother, since you passed away, I've been so lonely, you were my whole world; honest, good, tough, strong, funny, smart and soft, all in good measure and time. Now I'm doing what you asked me to do, and I'll keep going; I'll write everything down, everything I'm going through.

No. I'll write thoughts and experiences, also memories so that my children remember me as I am and not as the distorted figure that Mr. B. made me out to be. It's clear to me now that he never appreciated me. He'll never tell the truth about me. If he did, how would it make him look? I think I'm becoming stronger now, I know how to say exactly what I want and what I expect, and it doesn't matter to me if it doesn't sound realistic. If we're the ones creating reality, how can this be unrealistic?

I want a strong man, one who won't be negatively influenced by society and who's strong enough to stand by me no matter what. To love and never be ashamed to show love; one who doesn't suffer from low self-esteem or an over-inflated ego.

I want a man who gives without thinking about it and without ulterior motives. A man who doesn't look in the mirror all day, checking his 'cover' – rather what's inside him. I want the man by my side to love his children and his wife and, with great satisfaction in his heart, be happy to have them and them him; his loyalty will be absolute and his love unconditional. I don't think it's impossible.

Mr. B. will have to decide who he is, once and for all.

Yes. That's it! This is how it will be: all or nothing; it all depends on the will.

I don't want to compromise anymore, certainly not after everything that happened and especially after this wonderful summer. The children and I deserve the best, and if Mr. B. thinks otherwise, then his place is not at our side. Because we always thought he deserved the best, and that's why we loved him with all our hearts and wished the best for him.

I stood there on the deck wearing a light blue dress with little white and pink flowers. The fog covered the horizon, the sky and the earth, and yet, everything was clear to me. My dear children have only me. Me? I have to succeed for them.

"There you are, a little lady hiding in the fog," Nadav said.

"Did you find her?" asked Ari. "What's with the fog?!"

"Right? A rare sight," I said, "and in August, no less."

"You probably won't be able to leave us today," I heard Ben.

"It's really hard to leave you, dear people like you," I said.

"We're not going anywhere until they throw us out of here," Ari said.

"We'll be waiting for you! I heard Italy isn't something special anyway," Nadav continued.

"And you won't get rid of us so easily," Ari added.

I love you all very much. You can't put a price on what you have given us this summer. Although I wanted to say it, I stopped myself. I was afraid that the words would be too big and detract from the perfection of things as they are now, as they were during all summer. Instead, I smiled and said, "I want to wake the children so they too can enjoy this special morning, full of magic, before it disappears." We stood quietly, smiling and embarrassed, very happy. When I said I'd wake the children, it was as if I had given validity to the sense of family that we all shared this summer.

"Mom? Are you here?" asked Neil.

"Yes, honey, I'm here. I am coming to you," I said.

"Nell, Mom is here! I found her," Neil called to Nell.

"Make a wish, it seems you're doing well," said Nadav.

"For us too," said Ari.

"We're here, right? For you," said Ben.

"No matter what," I said and smiled. My heart skipped a beat.

"No matter what, sister," said Nadav, approaching and hugging me.

I was very excited; my heart was beating so hard. May we always feel this way, connected. Important to each other. My eyes sparkled with tears. It's good that there was fog; they won't notice and, if they do, they'll think it's because of the fog. I don't want them to know how emotional I am. I don't want them to feel obligated.

"Well, move over, you're not alone here," said Ari.

"Take a number, bro," Ben said it naturally, as if his friendship with Nadav and Ari had always been there. It warmed my heart.

"There's no need to fight over me," I said, letting go of Nadav, "I love you all, dear knights. Thank you, Sir Ariel." I bowed. "Sir Nadav," I continued and bowed. "And Sir Ben," I bowed again. "You are the best of friends; I wish you'd multiply; the world needs superheroes like you." I hugged Ari and Ben.

Nelly laughed a heartwarming, humble laugh. She understood the feeling in my words.

Neil smiled. He's still young but very intelligent and, in his own special way, he understood the spirit of what I said.

"Maybe we'll play hide-and-seek in the fog? Do we have time until the flight?" Nelly asked.

"A little," I replied.

"And that's enough time to play," Nadav said.

"You go hide, I'm the seeker," Ari said. Princes! One and all!

"You know, when I taught Nelly how to play hide-and-seek, she was almost three years old and, when I finished counting, I would ask, 'Where's Nelly?' And Nelly would say, 'Here. I'm here,' and would come out of hiding."

We all chuckled.

"There isn't a sweeter and more wonderful girl than you?!" I said, hugging and embarrassing her.

"A real sweetheart," Ben said.

"The sweetest," Ari added.

I love them very, very much and more for every word they say. I needed Nelly to hear those words, it was important to me that she be loved the way she deserves to be loved, the way I love her.

"And what about me, Mom? How was I?" asked Neil.

"I hid with you so you knew you didn't have to reveal where we were." I looked at Neil smiling, pulling him towards me to hug him as well.

I haven't had time to compliment Neil yet, and Nadav asked, "Sir Neil, the brave knight, shall we hide in the fog and startle Ari?" Neil laughed, understanding and cooperative. What a great soul my dear, dear Neil has.

It was a one-of-a-kind game. We didn't really have to hide, the fog hid us. It was funny and magical. It felt like we were playing in the sky, hiding among the clouds.

I thought we'd say our goodbyes to everyone at home, but everyone thought otherwise, and so it turned out that we arrived at the airport in two cars and not in a taxi as I had planned.

Nelly and Neil were very excited about the flight. It was their first time on a plane and, the truth is, they were also very much looking forward to seeing Mr. B. After all, he is their father and they love him. The children, who never knew what really happened, remembered him for the good years with him. Their excitement was contagious but I needed proof that the good years could still hold up. I couldn't allow us all to lose any more precious time. It was important for both of us to make sure that the foundations were fortified, stable, and that we wouldn't fall again.

I wanted it to be good, not just in my thoughts; I wanted it to be better than it was before the last two years, and for them to be forgotten. I wanted to know I wasn't wrong about Mr. B., that he just lost his mind for a while and he came back when he understood what he had done, understood how important we were to him and remembered that we were a family, although I was hurt and I wanted back what I thought I had.

We all said our goodbyes.

"Take care of each other," I said.

"We'll wait for you. Don't worry, we know how to recognize rare gems," Ari said.

"And we have no intention of losing them," Nadav added.

"Thank you for this wonderful summer, for being true friends." *So trustworthy and such very special people! I feel very blessed to have met you! That we met you,* I wanted to add but didn't. I didn't want them to feel committed. In the end, I didn't hold back: "You're all the best, irreplaceable," I said. How was it possible to go without telling them how wonderful they were?

Ben came toward me and handed me the last carry-on bag. "You are another reason to get up in the morning," he said as he hugged me to him. I knew it was very difficult for him to say those words. My heart almost burst. I appreciated him so much. He meant what he said and I was happier for him than for us. I realized how meaningful his words were. He felt he could trust us, he was able to rely on us, knows that we understand him truly and completely.

"You're one in a million. Your family is lucky to have you. Just because you don't see something doesn't mean it doesn't exist, right? You're a father every child would want and you are every woman's heart's desire. You are a wonderful person! We're honored to have met you. We won you this summer." I hugged him tight.

The children said goodbye again to Ari, Nadav and Ben, or, more accurately, Ari, Nadav and Ben said goodbye to the children again. It was hard for all of us to say goodbye.

I was glad that they connected like that, Ari Nadav and Ben. Ben won't be alone anymore.

We'll miss them.

If things work out with Mr. B. and everything goes back to the way it was, or even better, we will have them over together, just like we always loved to host. The warmth in our little house could contain more than it could hold, and everyone felt wonderful. There was no crowding, only warmth. And us? We really enjoyed pampering our guests, from the candles to a sumptuous meal, to special desserts that everyone loved. The compliments I repeatedly received were confirmation of the success of the effort.

Neil kept the box with the notepad from the treasure hunt with him, as did Nelly. Neil wanted me to write down the experiences he had this summer. Nelly also intended to as well; she already had a drawing of a window with a curtain, a flowerpot with flowers and a cloud in the sky that she drew in pencil and colored in very gently and tastefully with crayons that Ari, Nadav, and Ben had bought for her. They bought a set for Neil too. They both seemed so peaceful, empowered and loved. As wonderful as they are, they deserve to have only the best.

With heartache and many worries, but also with the hope that, if you want it, it can be done, I will board the plane to Italy with my dear children.

Me again:

The last bag I handed her, the briefcase, didn't end up on the plane. It was accidentally left on a chair in the café. Luckily, I went back for coffee before leaving the airport.

They returned from Italy a year later. We spoke several times on the phone while they were there. She had ambivalent feelings. From what I understood, he continued to make her feel bad about herself but it wasn't black and white anymore. There were moments when she felt he was the same man she loved and wanted to live her life with him 'until death do they part' but there were also moments when she wanted the divorce papers signed as soon as possible and to never see him again, or so she said. Again black and white, only this time the game between the two confused her. "If he loves me, he'll just throw away everything that happened as if it never did, and give me the sense of security I need to believe in us again, otherwise I'll understand that he doesn't love me."

She was right, in a way. When a man loves a woman, he does everything to make her know it. But their relationship had undergone a severe shake-up and not everyone is like her, she needs to understand, while she forces herself to stay in this situation. It's hard for her to act like nothing happened, like he wants to do, because he says one thing and does another, she says. How can you start fresh if he keeps picking at the scars? she says. Regrets, destructive thoughts, a struggle between good and evil, that's what they have and she doesn't want it. She wasn't ready for evil to triumph, so she could very easily dismiss his mistakes as if they never happened. She could honestly forget everything if she felt that he was one hundred percent with her and with the children, regretting his actions and loving her and the children, as she needs, as they need, as he showed her when they chose to get married. That's what makes her invincible. I told her, "He finds it hard to admit to himself that he ruined something so good because it makes him feel even worse about himself, makes him feel like he lost, that he's weak. I think he loves you very much but can't stand the fact that he hurt you. He prefers to think that the relationship wasn't successful in the first place, and that's how he can cope with the mistakes he's made. That's how he can justify it." I told her. "Give it more time and another chance if you still need to but, if you do, you also have to understand that not everything is black and white."

"Grey areas are confusing – they're gloomy and indecisive. It's either yes or no. Black or white, love or not love, making the effort or not. It's all a matter of choice," she said.

"There are things that take time and need to go through a process in order to reach their ideal state." I wanted to enlighten her through the butterfly's life trajectory, the way it crawls at first, progressing slowly, helplessly, and then becomes a cocoon. It seemed like it isn't going to get out of it and finally it turns into a beautiful insect, spreading its wings and flies away. I've saved it for some time in the future when it becomes harder. And it was clear to me that it would be harder for them. They are very different. I was divided: I wanted to help her save their relationship, for her sake, for the sake of the children, for every child needs a father to love and with whom to feel safe, who will be proud of him. On the other hand, I thought about how much more she deserves, how much more the children deserve – the best there is. I'm trying for her sake. I won't tell her what I really think. Every time I hear that she isn't doing well, I'd like to go back and remind her that she doesn't need him, that she should kick him out without thinking twice, she's thought enough, until she finally will have the strength to do it. But it has to be her decision. I don't want her to regret it, I don't want to be the one who made her do something she regrets, I want to be the most wonderful friend to her. Her safe place. Instead of saying it, I listened to her, to what she needed from me. I give it to her with my fists clenched. I'd punch him if he was in front of me.

"Maybe I'm just putting us all through unnecessary suffering," she said, but she sounded hesitant and not entirely sure of herself.

"You're in the gray area," I told her "otherwise you would have left."

"But his kisses and his touch and the magnetic feeling of connection that existed before is still there and that's why I don't want to leave. I didn't notice it until it was lost for a while. I want things to be good for him, for me, and for the children. It's a shame to waste one more day on disagreements or unnecessary arguments. I apologize, every conversation is about me. How are you, how do you feel? How are Nadav and Ari? We haven't spoken recently."

"I'm fine and Nadav and Ari are doing great. They're working on a soundtrack for a new movie."

I wasn't in the country when she came back, I had to go sort out some things. Then when I came back, she wasn't in the country; she was traveling with the children and kept it mysterious.

"I'll tell you, but not now," she said over the phone.

She returned six months later. She hadn't said anything, kept everything a secret.

In March, close to my birthday, we all met again, along with Nell and Neil, Nadav and Ari. The encounter taught us how connected we are, connected to each other, regardless of place and time, as if time had not passed and we were still at the house on the beach.

Everyone, in turn, talked about what they were going through, what they had accomplished, and the way they felt. But she surprised us all.

She bought everyone plane tickets to New York for the summer to see her play 'From Adam to Noah' which will premiere on Broadway. The word 'miracle' was used a lot; "It's a miracle they returned my call. It was a miracle that they agreed to take a risk and put it on a Broadway stage, a real miracle..." Nadav and Ari were speechless...

"And that's not all: I was approached by film studios in Los Angeles about an adaptation I wrote for The Beauty and the Beast, and they would like to work with me on it. We signed a contract," she said, so happy.

"You've accomplished a lot," Nadav said. "Wow! Wow, I have no words to tell you how happy I am for you."

"Yes, that's wonderful!" said Ari. "What a success!"

"I hope for you too..." she said.

"For us?" asked Nadav.

"You write music for movies and series. I'd like us to work together on this film. I wanted to do it with the play too, but you were busy. We could barely talk on the phone."

"Thanks, honey, but no. It won't be possible. Even now we're busy, full until May of 2025," Nadav said.

She was embarrassed but tried to hide it with a smile that didn't quite do the trick.

"Seriously?! Don't you know us already? Even if we didn't have the time, we would make time for you. Of course, we'd love to work with you!" Ari said.

"I can't stand you," she told Nadav. Nadav laughed and got up to hug her.

"Good to know you haven't changed," he said. "Don't you know by now there's nothing we won't do for you? You just have to ask."

"How did you do it? It sounds like a fantasy," Ari said.

"That's it, it's very strange. I sent the play and the adaptation of the film to the offices of two very large directors and filmmakers, and it ended up in the hands of completely different people. I lost my mind from happiness; no words came out except 'thank you, thank you, thank you, thank you and thank you and thank you again.'"

I chuckled.

She looked at me, stopped talking for a moment and said, "Funny. Right?"

"Yes. Yes." I replied.

"It doesn't matter to me how or what happened, the main thing is that they loved my work and it turned from a dream to reality," she said.

Nadav raised a toast and smiled. We understood what he meant, and we all raised our glasses wordlessly and smiled. For us, she was a dream and a reality.

In the summer we went to the premiere of her play. There were also three of her best friends; one of them came with her husband.

The play received excellent reviews.

She decided that the marriage wasn't good. The endless arguments. She had no idea what they were even about. There's too much distrust between them, mainly because of him, she said, he doesn't make her feel safe. She came to the conclusion that it's hard for him when people are happy, he has to burst their bubble. He's the only one who should be allowed to be happy. 'Practice what you preach' doesn't exist for him. Maybe it's all about control, he's the one who'll control when it's good and when it's bad, he'll decide when to be happy and when not to be, maybe he wants to drive her crazy because, despite everything she's been through with him, it hasn't corrupted her. In our conversation a week ago, she said, "You know, I think I'm close to making a decision. I've been thinking a lot about the Creation stories lately."

"Creation stories?" I asked. "What do you mean?"

"Those in Genesis One and Two: The Two Stories of Man's Creation."

"Isn't there only one?" I asked.

"No, there are two," she replied. She manages to surprise me every time. "I explained to Mr. B. that, in my opinion, these are two different types of relationships: Genesis 1 is a relationship that has wholeness and perfection; the relationship between the man and woman is one of equality, God created them together, male and female, and blessed them both equally.

The second type of relationship is one of ruler and the ruled, the one in Genesis 2. The relationship is unequal: man was created first and, after the animals, the woman was created because 'It is not good for man to be alone; I will make him a helper fit for him.' So even if she is in a higher position than him, because he could not have lived without her, or if he is in a higher position because she was created for him and only after the animals, either way, it is an unequal relationship. It's a bond of dominant and dominated and, therefore, doomed to failure because no one wants to be controlled. No one wants to be at a disadvantage. Such a situation leads to failure and expulsion from paradise, while the first relationship leads to heavenly life. That's why I consulted with you about everything, I told Mr. B., not because I couldn't decide on my own but because I wanted us to be equal, for the action to be ours, for us to evolve in a healthy way without anger or regret, without feeling as if one has lost or has been humiliated. I explained it to him, but again, he belittled me. He interprets my willingness to compromise as stupidity. It hurts us all. The children are starting to understand. It's hard to hide it from them anymore, and it hurts them a lot. He doesn't respect me in front of them and they feel that he doesn't respect them either, and so he fills them with details that they shouldn't hear, time and time again. When we're alone, he is wonderful to me and, in front of them, he is very rough and rude." She paused for a moment and then said: "Nadav's on call waiting."

"It's okay, I'll wait. Or would you rather get back to me later?" I asked. "I also have Ari on call waiting," I said.

Ari and Nadav tried to arrange a meeting with us before going to Canada. They wanted to meet this evening.

They want to travel to North America before they start working on the music for the film. They always travel before creating a new soundtrack as travel promotes their writing and creation. We set up a meeting. In the evening, she came with the children, Neil and Nelly.

Later in the evening, I said, "I thought about our conversation earlier today and it was very interesting to take the two creation stories and see them as two types of relationships. I don't think I would have come to that realization," I said.

"What kinds of relationships?" asked Nadav and, after she finished sharing it with him and Ari, Ari said: "You surprised me. Very interesting. I've never thought about it that way."

"So what you're saying is that inequality leads to expulsion from life in paradise?" added Ari after a moment of pondering.

"Yes. Exactly," she replied, "and that's why it's a relationship that is destined to fail."

"I thought the woman was to blame for the expulsion," Nadav said.

"Man, according to Genesis Two, was created before the woman and he was responsible for the garden: to work and guard it along with the prohibition not to eat the fruit from the Tree of Knowledge. The woman ate first and gave it to Adam, but he didn't argue or get angry with her for eating the forbidden fruit, so he ate it, too. When they were questioned, the man immediately blamed the woman, wanting her to be punished for his actions. Heaven is supposed to be a place for good people, isn't it? Man didn't come off looking good when he didn't take responsibility for his actions, even more so when he didn't protect the woman who, when she was created, said, "This is now bone of my bones and flesh of my flesh; she shall be called 'woman,' for she was taken out of man." I would expect a man to ask God for forgiveness for the mistake, for his wife as well, and to pledge not to repeat such a mistake again, to express remorse. Maybe then the man would deserve to stay in paradise."

"But still, she's the one who gave him the apple. She didn't have to make him fall," Ari said.

"Not an apple," she said.

"Not an apple?" asked Ari.

"No. It's written 'the fruit of the tree of knowledge of good and evil," she replied.

"Which school did you go to in Australia?" Nadav asked.

We all laughed.

"Is that the reason the fruit had a different shape in the play? I thought you were trying to give the apple a different look, one that would differ from the other apples, special to paradise. I didn't know it wasn't an apple either. Interesting. The woman, why did she have to spoil it?" said Nadav.

"True, she didn't have to bring him the fruit, she brought it because she didn't die after eating it and, apparently, she thought the snake was right. But him? It was he who received the prohibition from God, he was the one who worked the garden, he knew very well that eating the fruit of the Tree of Knowledge was forbidden, and yet, he ate from it! Think about it, if it were today, what kind of relationship could they have when the woman knows that her partner didn't protect her and even wanted her to be punished, and thus save himself, that he didn't love her enough to help her get out of the problem she finds herself in and not out of ill intent. In any case, she didn't try to harm him. Nevertheless, she ate the fruit first. If she was evil she would have given it to him first, to check whether the snake was right or not, but she checked it herself first. And when she didn't die, as Adam told her would happen if they ate from it, then she brought it to him as well."

We all sat quietly for a moment, stunned. I don't think any of us would have thought of it that way if she hadn't said it.

"Interesting," Nadav said.

"Very interesting," we said, admiring together.

She always manages to draw you into things you wouldn't have thought of on your own, had she not, in her own interesting way, brought up.

"When you talk about it, it sounds logical," Nadav said. "What woman would agree to continue a relationship in which the man is a coward, doesn't take responsibility, blames her?"

She looked down for a moment, Nadav, who obviously didn't mean it, reflected her situation. She looked up, her eyes sparkled slightly, took a sip of her drink as if she was struggling to swallow the pain.

I saw Nadav's look and how, for a moment, he flashed Ari his gaze. I think Nadav and Ari understood a long time ago that there was a problem. Maybe even when we were at the beach house, but they didn't say anything because she didn't say anything. They never mentioned anything to me either, because we all earnestly wanted to protect her. They respected her wishes not to say anything, but made sure that she and the children had nothing but the best, that they would feel loved all the time, and the truth is that they were loved in our hearts anyway, not out of compassion or need, but because we put them there, forever. Now, I'm sure of it, Nadav and Ari got confirmation of their suspicions; they also saw her swallowing the pain.

"Because I believe that this is indeed logical, and the book teaches us what we should pay attention to. The story teaches us that temptation is everywhere. It's not in vain that it begins with food. If we don't guard what we received as a gift, which takes work, we won't be able to return to the good place we were before we fell into temptation. And even more so, if we add insult to injury and don't express remorse, everything will be lost forever." I understood why she said these words. Ari and Nadav understood as well.

"Why did He have to put that damn tree in the garden in the first place?!" said Ari. We all chuckled. It was clear to me and, surely, to Nadav, why he said it.

"Why test?" he continued.

"Not to test. It's about free will," she replied.

"So what's the lesson of the story? That if there's free will, you'd choose evil? It seems that evil was there from the beginning, regardless of whether or not they ate from the tree; the snake," Nadav said. It felt like he and Ari were trying to distract her from the issue by pulling her into another part of the story. "Yes. There's free will. There's temptation. If there were regret, responsibility, the damn tree wouldn't have been a problem, they probably would have stayed in paradise. I believe the main message is that an unequal relationship is doomed to fail. The relationship of Genesis One is harmonious and successful."

The evening was very pleasant, the special peaceful feeling we had in the beach house was still there, and it was clear to all of us that it would remain forever. It's impossible to take it away from us.

We were the last to leave. Before I said goodbye to her, I asked if she wasn't busy tomorrow, we could go with the kids to Disneyland or anywhere else they wanted to go. She told me, "I have a meeting tomorrow in the studio about Beauty and the Beast. Can we be in touch afterward? It'll be very nice to take a walk together. I'll finally see the studios. I planned on taking the kids with me, so that would work out fine."

Right after she left and, of course, after wishing her the best of luck, I knew it'd be better if I arrived at the studios before she did the next day.

She was early and arrived before I did. I couldn't do anything about it.

I sat on a bench across the lawn in front the entrance to the studios and waited for her to come out.

She approached me with a serious look on her face. I stood up.

"The sign at the entrance... it took me a few minutes... do you own the studios?"

"Can I explain," I said, "may I?" she waited quietly.

"I read the play and the film adaptation, which were in the briefcase you forgot at the cafe. I went back there because I wanted to make sure again that you were okay, but you had already left. I bought coffee and that's how I found it. I wanted to send it to you in a box, I was already at the post office, but I changed my mind. I opened it; I don't normally do things like that, but I wanted to see what I could do so you wouldn't feel like you were alone in everything that happened. I apologize. I opened the suitcase, found the play and the script. In my opinion, they were excellent. I gave the script to the studios, the play I gave to a friend and he loved it." She still stood in front of me quiet, serious, attentive.

"I only opened the door, you did everything else completely on your own. Why didn't I tell you? Because I didn't know how to explain to you why I opened the suitcase and read your writings. I apologize for the way I did it, but you're so wonderful and special to me, you have no idea how much, and you deserve the best. I wanted the best for you."

She sat down and put her hand on the bench, motioning for me to sit next to her.

After a moment of silence and a wandering look between the vegetation and me, she said, "Do you know which fairytale I loved the most when I was little?" as she looked me straight in the eyes: "Cinderella! Do you know why? Because Cinderella was good and beautiful but defenseless and the stepmother knew it and took advantage of it, made her someone who wouldn't be noticed and made her life difficult so she'd lose hope. The stepmother could not stand Cinderella for all the wonderful qualities she had, which she and her ugly daughters lacked. She shattered her last glimmer of hope when she wouldn't let her go to the ball. The good fairy appeared and, against all odds, she came to the ball and was the most beautiful of them all, the prince wanted only her. He then searched the entire kingdom for the girl whose foot matched the shoe left behind and, even though she was wearing rags when he found her, he still saw the same woman he had fallen in love with at the ball. Neither the stepmother's tricks nor Cinderella's ragged looks could take away what he felt for her at the ball. So romantic, I could listen to that story again and again. It filled my heart with joy. A happy ending. All's well it ends well.

"You, dear Ben, gave me the glass slipper! You saw beyond the rags," she paused for a moment. "There's no other like you, Ben!" she put her hand on mine. I held hers back. "I thank you so much and love..." suddenly she stopped. Her voice weakened with the last word and tears stopped her from continuing. She made an effort to stop them from falling.

"Me, too," I said after a moment, completely serious. I saw how embarrassed she was so I smiled cautiously, very carefully. I wanted her to know that there was intention behind those words.

"For some time now I've been writing episodes for a comedy series. Maybe I'll make Mr. B. the main character. He doesn't lack humor but he lacks tact, he doesn't think about who'll get hurt and, the truth is, that he has another side. Besides his bad side, he really makes you laugh. It will be perfect. He's the modern Archie Bunker."

"Yes, I think he'll be very successful at this, the audience will love him and that will remove his bitterness and soften his cynicism. He'll be happy. Therefore, it is the right time to say goodbye. The children have also grown up. They can't be obligated to shared custody. They'll decide where they want to be," she said, and an expression of relief appeared on her face. How much light her face radiated! How beautiful she was at that moment, more than ever, you could see that her heart was free.

"He's lucky to have you."

"You think? Because sometimes I feel like maybe he'd be better off with another woman, who would have probably left him after the betrayal, and that would have made him feel good that he got what he deserved; maybe the struggle would have done him good when he tried to make amends. I took it from him when I came back to him after the mistake he made. Enough. Enough. I don't want to confuse myself again. I'm confusing myself again. I think I understand the gray area."

"Another woman would have left him miserable to pay for what he did, and when she'd succeeded as well as you did, she'd be filled with nothing but victory, enjoying its taste, raising another glass to the defeat of the terrible husband she got rid of. It would've been the last nail in his coffin, and it would have been a burial, believe me, from which he'd never recover. You gave him another way, one that he might never admit to, how much you helped him and how wonderful you are. Forgive me, I know it will not satisfy you, but he's not in a place where he can say something you'll feel good about, when he feels like such a scum inside. You gave him a real chance; you saved his life and his relationship with the children." I paused for a moment. "I don't know how you do it. How do you have all this good energy? Forgiveness? Love? Compassion? And with such modesty?! You are a special and good person, you deserve all the good that there is. I feel blessed meeting you and being your friend."

"Love your neighbor as yourself, right?" She smiled a captivating smile.

"You know, your office, the big and beautiful one at the end of the hallway, has been empty for a long time. I'm sure your presence in the company is greatly missed. There are still many people to make happy. I'll help you come back if you want." she said cautiously with a smile, her eyes once again filled with enough light and strength to rebuild an entire world.

"Media is this wonderful thing that touches people's hearts, inspires them, opens the door to a wonderful world of music, colors, ideas and endless possibilities."

I smiled. My loss will always remain in my heart. There's something about her, the way she looks at you, the way she says things and her energy that makes you whole, that makes you feel okay with what you feel, what you do and who you are. I knew that she won't want to take the place of the ones that were and still are dear to me; she'd respect my need for what I hold onto, she'd maintain this love and bring out the best in me, making me feel like I belonged, was needed, loved and understood. She won't be threatened by the memory that lives in my heart because she understands. She understands the meaning of loyalty.

"I wanted to ask the owner of the studio to postpone the film until 2025. A little far off, isn't it? Do you think he'll agree?"

I wanted to answer her immediately, of course, 'Do you even need to ask? You just need to say the word,' but I didn't get the chance, as she immediately justified:

"I have a reason. I found the Beauty, but she hasn't reached the right age yet." she smiled, and her eyes were embarrassed.

"Of course. You don't have to explain. It's clear that she's the Beauty. So clear."

"Thank you. Thank you so much for understanding me," she said, tears streaming from her eyes. She hugged me tightly.

"Everything is so wonderful. I wanted so much for life to be simple, good, easy, and wonderful. Thank you for making this possible for me. I can never thank you enough."

She is wonderful and I would like to give her everything she needs to make her feel happy, every single moment. I can't promise her that life will be simple, good, easy and wonderful because who better than I knows that there are things that happen that don't depend on us. But I can promise her that I am completely committed, that I will do whatever is in my power to make things as simple and easy, as good and wonderful as possible for her.

Maybe one day, she will be ready for more. I would like there to be more but, until then, I will be the best friend I can be and, even if she doesn't want more, I will be there for her.

She can trust me. I'll keep her from changing. I'll be by her side for whatever she wants and, if she stumbles, I'll be there to hold her up, I'll go as far as she needs and I'll make sure to remind her how wonderful she is all the time.

P.S.
I changed the children's names in her writings and didn't mention her name to protect her privacy, because today they are all famous people.

Ben.

Printed in Dunstable, United Kingdom

68743678R00092